D1706779

AMY OPPENHEIM

PRETTY INNOCENT GIRLS

a novel

Copyright © 2021 by Amy Oppenheim

All rights reserved. No part of this publication may be
reproduced, stored or transmitted in any form or by any
means, electronic, mechanical, photocopying, recording,
scanning, or otherwise without written permission from the
publisher. It is illegal to copy this book, post it to a website,
or distribute it by any other means without permission.

This novel is entirely a work of fiction. The names,
characters and incidents portrayed in it are the work of the
author's imagination. Any resemblance to actual persons,
living or dead, events or localities is entirely coincidental.

Amy Oppenheim asserts the moral right to be identified as
the author of this work.

First edition

Cover art by Xavier Comas

This book was professionally typeset on Reedsy.
Find out more at reedsy.com

For Jenny Lorber

"Those we love never truly leave us."
– Harry Potter and the Cursed Child

Contents

Acknowledgement

First and foremost, I want to thank the amazing people in my life who've supported me, not only through life in general, but also through this process of completing my story. A huge thank you to my friends and first beta readers, Mandy, Kelly, Nicole, Jennie and Nick, who gave me honest, important and sometimes hilarious feedback as I developed the story.

Next, I owe substantial credit to my dear friend Makenna for the marathon brainstorming sessions, brilliant contributions to the story, constant encouragement and wicked smart editing. I am eternally grateful for all the many ways you helped me take this over the finish line.

I'd also like to give a shout out to my sister, Cindy, for being my sounding board, emotional support sibling and cheerleader throughout the turbulent 2020 pandemic, which also afforded me the free time to finally write a book.

Chapter 1

The first time she fantasized about cheating on her husband was the day she and Craig moved into their new place by the beach in Ventura, California.

It was an obscenely hot day, and the humidity made it impossible to carry the heavy boxes inside. Every time she'd get a good grip on the cardboard, her sweaty skin would send it sliding out of her arms and onto the ground.

"GODDAMMIT," she screamed as another one crashed down on her feet. She kicked the box off her and wiped sweat from her forehead with the back of her hand.

"What's wrong?" Craig called out from the driveway.

"Just dropped another box on my toes," she shot back angrily.

"It wasn't the 'breakable' one, was it? I think that's our wedding china."

"I didn't have time to see which box *fell on me*. But thanks for your concern."

Craig stepped into the doorway and looked at his wife lovingly. "I'm sorry. That was insensitive. Are you ok?"

His words made her soften a little. She sighed. "Yeah, I'm fine. Just moving stress."

"I know," he agreed. "But after we're settled, you'll have all the time in the world to decompress and relax."

She nodded and returned to the truck. As she lifted a less intimidating looking box, she felt Craig move in behind her, putting his arm around her waist and pulling her sweaty body into his.

"Blake," he whispered. "I love you."

She smiled and closed her eyes as he kissed her salty neck. He ran his hands up and down her waist, sliding them under her tank top and giving her breasts a light squeeze.

"I know this transition isn't easy for you," he continued quietly in her ear. "But it will be good for us. I promise. We're finally gonna be so comfortable that your gorgeous ass doesn't have to work anymore."

Her smile faded.

"Plus," he continued, running his fingers through her hair. "Now you'll finally have time to focus on your painting and yoga—the ocean is just down the street."

She rolled her eyes at the condescending remark and wiggled out of his embrace to storm back into the house, leaving him and the boxes behind. *He can handle unloading himself.*

Plugging in her Bluetooth speaker in the kitchen, she opened Spotify in her phone and put on her favorite Glass Animals song to try and drown out the stress of moving day.

She wandered out into the backyard and sat in the shade on the back porch steps to cool off, the music fading into the background. She gazed out at their enormous backyard, filled with lush orange trees and beautiful flowers, bees buzzing everywhere. While the neighborhood they moved into wasn't her idea of a great place to live, it had potential. California real estate prices were insane, even more so this close to the ocean. And the area they'd chosen, though adjacent to the high-end beach community and still rather pricey, was considered the "rough" part of Ventura. But Craig had insisted it was slowly becoming gentrified and that this was the perfect time to buy real estate there, as the value of the neighborhood was projected to increase drastically in 10 years. He'd suggested they fix up the house and eventually rent it out once they could afford something nicer, which had in turn caused a massive argument. She'd protested that it was wrong to try and "gentrify" a neighborhood, essentially rendering it unaffordable to those who'd lived there for years, forcing them out of their homes and further inland. But Craig didn't seem concerned with that. He wanted a good deal on a great investment. He'd also reminded her that this was the "poor ghetto," not the "dangerous ghetto." And she'd told him that was the whitest privileged thing she'd ever heard him say. But in the end, she'd agreed to the location because it meant they'd live five minutes from the beach and still be able to afford a decent house.

As she quieted herself in the backyard, she heard male voices coming from the house next door. Curious about her new neighbors, she looked toward the fence between their houses, and saw there was a sizeable hole in it which offered her a perfect view of their yard.

Ugh, fixer uppers. Why didn't Craig repair that? He'd been flying out regularly for the past two months to settle into his new job and get the house ready for them to move in, fixing up broken appliances and repainting the interior walls. And yet somehow, he missed this gaping hole?

As she continued to eavesdrop and peer into the fence's gap, she saw two men in jeans and what appeared to be matching leather vests *(how can they stand that on this hot day?)* laughing

3

at a third man's joke. Something about a woman he'd slept with who had inverted nipples.

"I half expected her to have an inverted pussy."

"You mean like a small dick?" The captive, crude audience chuckled.

She watched one of them take a swig from a bottle and then throw the empty glass into a container across the yard, where it shattered loudly. Then their voices lowered, and they inched closer toward one another. It appeared the topic had become more serious. Since she was already leaning as far in as she could from her spot on the porch steps, she walked closer to the fence to hear better.

But just as she approached the fence, she was startled by the abrasive sound of a motorcycle roaring down the street and then pulling into the side yard toward where the three men were standing. They all stopped talking as the motorcycle—still loudly rumbling—pulled all the way into the backyard and its rider shut the engine off.

"Hayden, bro! You're back already," one of the guys called to the man now dismounting the motorcycle. "We thought you'd be gone until next weekend."

"What, planning on throwing a party for your little school friends while Daddy's out of town?" Hayden shot back, which made the rest of the group laugh.

As Hayden stood from his motorcycle, she got a better look at him. He appeared to be in his late 30s, and as he took his helmet off, she saw he had long, dark, beach-waved hair that looked like it hadn't been washed in several days. When he smiled at his friends, she noticed his dimples and strong jawline, combined with piercing blue eyes cradled in dark lashes. He was...beautiful.

"Blake, what are you doing out here?" Craig yelled from the back door, startling her, and sending her flying into the air.

"Just...checking out the backyard!" she called back.

Hayden and his friends looked up from their group as they heard this exchange and turned their focus to the new couple moving in next door.

They walked closer to the fence. She could see that their leather vests had something on the back of them, which looked like a skull with crossbones wearing a bandana face covering and a cowboy hat. She wondered if they were in one of those motorcycle clubs. Like *Sons of Anarchy* or something.

"Do we have new neighbors?" Hayden asked, looking only at her. He flexed his arms under his white t-shirt, accentuating his many tattoos.

"Hey, man, I'm Craig Davis," Craig answered before she could respond. "And this is my wife, Blake." He walked over to the fence with an outstretched hand, ready to politely meet the neighbors.

But Hayden and his friends just stood there, clearly having no intention of shaking hands. When Craig finally realized this, he dropped his own hand and smiled awkwardly.

Hayden looked them both up and down, saying nothing.

Finally, after several seconds of awkward silence, one of the men stepped forward, a tall skinny guy in his early 20s with red hair and freckled skin.

"I'm Red," he said with a tinge of embarrassment at the obvious nickname.

"These guys here are Elvis and Dave." He nodded toward the men he'd been joking around with. "And, this is Hayden," he said, pointing to the beautiful motorcycle rider.

Hayden continued to stare directly at her as his friend made

5

the introductions. She felt uncomfortable under his inappropriate gaze.

"You should really get this hole fixed," she said, realizing she'd been silent and needed to say something. "I can see into your whole backyard through it."

Hayden laughed. "Well, the last people who lived here smoked crack and pretty much kept to themselves. Now that we have more *outdoorsy* neighbors, I'll look into filling that hole." His lips curled into a smirk as he said *filling that hole*, still looking directly into her eyes.

She felt a jolt in her gut, like butterflies. Craig didn't seem to notice the implication. "Well, it's good to meet you all. We just moved here from Phoenix. Got a deal on this house, and now I know why! Crackheads, huh? Well, cheap real estate always comes with a price. Good thing I have Blake here to help get it fixed up and looking homey."

She was mortified by Craig's rambling on about their personal lives. Something about their new neighbors made her feel uncomfortable, like they needed to be careful what they said to them. Or maybe it was just the way that Hayden stared at her so blatantly, and in front of her oblivious husband.

"Alright, we'll let you get back to your day now," she chimed in to shut Craig up and end the awkward interaction.

"Nice meeting you, *Davises*," Hayden said playfully, still only looking at her.

She and Craig went back inside to work on unpacking.

Later that night, she was itching to get the sweat and grime of moving day off her, so she unpacked her toiletries and told Craig she planned to take a nice, long, hot shower.

While she washed the day out of her hair, her mind wandered back to Hayden. What was it about this grungy man on a motorcycle that had her so on edge? She didn't even like riding on the backs of motorcycles—especially after falling off of one in college with that idiot Steve she'd dated. Was it the way Hayden looked at her like she was a snack? She normally abhorred being objectified, but somehow, she found herself enjoying that he saw her as a sex object.

As she thought about this, she continued washing her body and found herself slipping into an intimate state, touching herself in the hot, soapy water as she thought about Hayden... about what his rough calloused hands would feel like on her soft skin. It was the first time she'd felt sexual in months.

The next morning, Craig went to work, leaving her home alone for the day to work on unpacking and setting up the house. As she brewed coffee and made a list of things to accomplish that day, she found her resentment toward Craig intensifying with each mundane house task she wrote out on her *"This is why I drink wine"* sassy notepad, which her best friend Jasmine had given her when they'd previously worked together.

She already missed her old life. Her friends, her career—an exciting job in public relations—her whole world that was uprooted for this new job. *For Craig's new fucking job.*

Things hadn't always been so tense between them. Their friends used to be envious of the annoyingly sweet romance they'd had when they first started dating, and even after they got married. Craig was always the life of the party. Everyone loved being around him and he had this magical ability to make everyone he met feel special, like they were important in their own unique way. That had been one of the charms that roped her in early on—Craig saw her as the witty, intelligent bombshell she'd always wanted to be. She felt lucky that he'd chosen her over all the other women who were equally enchanted by him. And while he feigned an endearing lack of awareness about his effect on the opposite sex, she knew deep down he reveled in it. But they had this rare chemistry that just seemed to work. They'd occasionally have arguments like all couples do, but never anything major enough to raise a red flag.

It wasn't until maybe a year after the wedding that Craig started to change. It wasn't an overnight transformation, but rather a slow and steady progression into a less charming version of himself. Where he had previously praised and encouraged her career growth and independence, he began pushing for a family and for her to ultimately become a "full-time mother," which he believed was the way a "mother was supposed to behave." This was all brand-new information to her when it revealed itself during an argument one day. She never knew he felt that way before they got married. And by then, it was too late to back out. They were legally bound.

But when Craig's boss introduced him to the horse races, that was when the drama really flared up. What started out as a fun approach to entertaining clients gradually morphed into a weekend hobby, which progressed into daily secret afternoon outings. Blake had been blindly unaware of this headway until her debit card was declined at the grocery store one day. After several uncomfortable conversations, Craig had agreed to seek help for what appeared to be a fixable problem.

Things improved, but Blake was still uneasy, still hesitant to trust. Her oblivious bubble had been burst, and it would be hard to go back to the way things had been. Craig was also still around the same people every day, still spending time with the boss who'd introduced him to the races in the first place. But he worked in finance, so when he told her he'd fixed everything

8

and that they were ok, she was determined to believe him. She *had* to believe him.

Nonetheless, when the opportunity arose for Craig to take a new job out in California, there was a part of her that felt it might be the opportunity they needed to start fresh. She didn't want to leave her life behind, but she also didn't resist quite as hard as she may have otherwise if things had been great in Phoenix. Maybe some separation from the bad influences would be good for him, good for their marriage.

So, she'd ended up on this journey with him to start over in Central Coast California, with promises of giving her the life she'd always dreamed of—living by the beach and spending more time painting and enjoying life. What Craig didn't realize, however, was that she also needed purpose, work that could stimulate her educated brain. And now she'd abandoned her bustling 1.6 million population in Phoenix for this new chapter in Ventura, with its modest population of just over 100,000. This small-town housewife life was not what she'd pictured for herself. And every time she'd tried to have an honest conversation with him about it, he'd pet her head condescendingly and brush her off, focusing on pursuing his own dream.

When she'd told Jasmine about her plans to resign and move for Craig's new job, Jasmine had feigned excitement and support, but she could see right through it. She saw the judgment of "oh, you've become one of *those* women now" in her eyes. But she'd made her decision and felt the right thing to do was to see it through. They were in their early 30s now after all, so the clock was ticking. Everyone kept telling her so, at least. What she didn't expect was how angry she'd feel toward Craig every day since she'd made the decision.

To distract herself, she turned on her favorite podcast, *My Favorite Murder,* as she put away dishes in the new kitchen cabinets. She'd thrown on her comfiest yoga pants and piled her long, blonde hair into a bun on top of her head for a day of setting up shop while catching up on her guilty pleasure: true crime stories. She zoned out in her chores, laughing along with podcast hosts Karen and Georgia as they discussed the famous Swiss Cheese Pervert, a serial flasher who liked to stick his penis inside the holes of Swiss cheese and showcase it to unsuspecting women.

As the episode ended, she heard the thunderous sound of several motorcycles pulling into the driveway next door. Curious, she walked over to the kitchen window facing their yard and peered through the curtains.

Hayden, Red, and two other men she didn't recognize, but who were wearing the same vests with the skulls with wings, were pulling their bikes into the driveway. As they dismounted and walked toward the front door, Elvis opened the door and nodded at them, ready for them to enter. A black car pulled into the driveway behind the men with their bikes, and two more men got out of the front of the car, walking around to the back of it.

What she saw next shocked her.

The two men popped the trunk and pulled another man out of it. The man had a gag over his mouth and his hands were bound behind him with zip ties. The bound and gagged man was kicking and fighting, but the other men jumped in to help forcefully carry him into the house.

Just as they were about to shut the door, Hayden did a quick scan around the street to make sure no one was watching, and then his eyes locked onto hers in her window.

She gasped and shut the curtain abruptly. *Shit.*

Oh my god. Did they just...kidnap someone? She paced the room as she took deep breaths and tried to make sense of what she'd just seen. And what Hayden had just seen her see. *Maybe if I just poke my head out back and spy through the fence, I can make sense of it.*

Tiptoeing onto her back porch steps, she hid behind a large wooden beam and watched in horror as the bikers dragged the bound man into their backyard. On the other side of their house, there was a precariously steep hill that shot high into the sky, so the only view into their backyard was from her own property.

The bikers took turns punching the man in the face and stomach, until he crumpled to the ground in muffled screams. Once he was on the pavement, they kicked and stomped his entire body until he was no longer screaming through his gag. The man finally lay still, and she watched as two bikers grabbed him by the arms, one by the legs, carrying him into a giant garage-sized shed at the edge of the backyard. A few minutes later, they re-emerged from the shed, sans bound man, and walked casually back into the big house.

Once everyone was inside, she became aware of herself and realized she'd been holding her breath the entire time. She let out a panicked exhale as she ran back into her house. When she was safely inside with the door locked, she clutched the kitchen counter and bent her face over the sink, taking deep breaths. *Who the hell are these people?*

She heard the black car and a couple of the motorcycles start their engines and pull out of the driveway, peeling away down the street.

She spent the next 10 minutes having an internal argument with herself about whether to call the police. On the one hand, she had just witnessed something heinous and obviously illegal, and there was a man who may be dead or dying locked up in that shed. She should try to help him. But on the other hand, something about this group...this gang...gave her pause about turning them in. Maybe they were dangerous. Maybe it would be in her best interest to just pretend she never saw anything and try to go back to normal. What was it the real estate agent had said to them about living on The Avenue? *If you don't bother them, they won't bother you.*

She glanced at the clock—2 p.m. *It's airport rules when you don't have a job, right?* She reached into the cabinet where she'd been organizing before this nightmare event had transpired and grabbed a wine glass. Walking over to one of their wine crates on the floor by the laundry room, she reached in and pulled out a bottle of Pinot Noir, uncorked, poured, and dove in headfirst.

At 7 p.m., she woke up, startled, to the jarring sound of Craig opening the front door. As he entered the living room to come greet her, she sat up on the couch and did a quick scan of the room. The now completely empty wine bottle and empty wine glass were out on full shame display on the coffee table next to her.

Craig eyed the empty bottle and then his wife. "I see you had yourself a little party today."

"Yeah, just felt like enjoying some wine after setting up the kitchen earlier," she responded, embarrassed.

"Looks like you really enjoyed it. Your lips and teeth are a nice shade of purple," he teased. "Bummer you didn't leave any for me!"

"I can open another bottle if you want some," she offered. She contemplated telling him what she'd witnessed that day.

But then Craig caught her off guard with what he said next.

"No. Right now, I just want you." He joined her on the couch, leaning in to kiss her wine-stained lips, and gently stroke her face with his hand, moving a loose strand of blonde hair behind her ear. She looked into his eyes, really looked, for the first time in a while, and remembered why she'd fallen for him. He was handsome in the most conventional way. Perfect lips, big, bright, brown eyes, a great head of hair (she'd worried he'd go bald like his dad, but so far there wasn't so much as a receding hairline). And he'd been growing out his beard recently, which she found to her surprise that she liked. It made him look like a sexy lumberjack.

Their kissing quickly escalated as he shoved his hand down her yoga pants and explored her, playing with her while kissing her neck and shoulders. She let out a satisfied moan. *No need to tell him about the badly beaten prisoner next door right now, I guess.* They had sex that night for the first time in a month.

Chapter 2

In the morning, Craig walked over to her side of the bed, fully dressed for work, and kissed her forehead. He smelled fresh, a minty-soapy combination. She, on the other hand, could taste how bad her morning breath was, so she refrained from opening her mouth to say anything, and instead just smiled up at him.

"I'm really happy we got to christen the new place last night, my sleepy little lush." He stood up straight before adding, "Just a heads up, I have to work late tonight and then I'm going to a meeting afterward, so don't worry about dinner. I'll text you when I have an idea what time I'll be home."

For some reason, "don't worry about dinner," made her seethe again. What, just because she was no longer working, she now was responsible for feeding him dinner every night? And was this a dig about the previous night where she'd had a bottle of wine for dinner, and he had to come home to a passed-out wife? Maybe she was reading into things too much, as usual. Maybe she was just being sensitive. Ever since Craig had started going to meetings back in Phoenix, she worried that his newfound disease-awareness would make him judgmental about other potentially addictive substances. But drinking had never really been his thing, so maybe she was just projecting her own insecurities onto him.

She waved goodbye and waited until she heard him close and lock the front door before getting out of bed. There was more work to do around the house, but all she could think about was the possibly dead or badly injured man in the shed in the backyard next door. And about the men—her neighbors—who had just casually kidnapped and brutally beaten this man in the middle of a Tuesday in broad daylight. Weren't they worried about people seeing? Weren't they worried about getting caught?

To try to maintain some self-control, she closed all the curtains and blinds on windows that faced the neighboring house. She needed to stop spying and focus on her own life. But as she walked around with artwork and pictures, measuring, and planning where to hang them, she caught herself drifting back to the memory of the previous day. Was that man still alive? *Did I do the right thing not calling the police? Should I tell Craig?*

But something inside her kept urging her to keep her mouth shut. Finally, she couldn't stand it anymore, and sat down at her kitchen table, pulling out her laptop to do some Googling. Phrases flew out of her fingertips: "California motorcycle clubs," "leather vest with skull and bandana," "motorcycle gangs."

What she saw unsettled her and made her heart race. Somehow, she'd stumbled onto the Army of Outlaws Wikipedia page. She sat back in her chair. The insignia shown on the page looked just like the one she'd seen them wear, but she hadn't gotten close enough to the backs of any of them to see what the writing said. Could they really be part of this infamous motorcycle club? According to Wikipedia, they were considered organized crime.

And if that were the case, they'd probably have connections with the local police anyway. *Best to keep my mouth shut.*

A loud knock at the front door made her jump out of her chair, slamming her laptop shut in defense. She inched toward the front entrance and yelled, "Who is it?"

"Police. Do you have a minute to answer a few questions?"

Her heart skipped a beat. Why would a police officer be at her door? *Shouldn't he be knocking on the neighbors' door?*

Her obsession with true crime and self-proclaimed status as a *murderino*, a term coined by the fans of the *My Favorite Murder* podcast used to describe regular citizens who fancied themselves amateur crime experts and sleuths, made her hesitant to open the door for someone claiming to be police. She made a mental note to tell Craig they needed to install a chain lock deadbolt. She took a deep breath and bravely unlocked and opened the door. A slender, Hispanic man with sunken eyes and an angular jawline stood in front of her, dressed in a navy suit.

"Good afternoon, ma'am. Thanks for speaking with me. I'm hoping to ask you a few questions about a disturbance that was reported yesterday."

"Sure," she said, heart pounding. *Why isn't he in uniform if he's police?* "But would you mind showing me your badge first?"

The police officer raised an eyebrow. "Been watching a lot of *Law & Order*, have you? I guess it's good you know your rights." He smirked as he pulled his badge out and held it up to her condescendingly. She saw the word "Detective" on his badge. *Ah, fancy cop.* She nodded, and then stepped out onto the front porch to join him, leaving her front door open.

"So, like I said, we got a report yesterday of an altercation outside a gas station a few blocks away. Seems a group of thugs on motorcycles beat up a man trying to pump gas, and they may have taken the man with them in a black sedan—possibly a VW of some sort. Security footage showed the group taking off in the direction of this neighborhood, and, given the colorful history of some of your neighboring residents and their motorcycles," he glanced over toward the house next door, "I'm making the rounds here to see if anyone saw anything."

"I just moved in," she said, not sure what was going to come out of her mouth. "Like two days ago. I don't know any of my neighbors yet."

"Ah, well welcome to the neighborhood then. Didn't mean to scare you with the 'colorful history' thing. I'm sure you'll be just fine here."

She smiled back awkwardly.

"So. Did you?" he asked.

"Did I what?"

"See anything yesterday?"

"Oh, sorry. No, I didn't see anything like that. I've just been unpacking." She shrugged her shoulders.

"Alright no worries. Thanks for your time then. Hey, will you please give me a call if you do see or think of anything unusual that could help us?" He handed her a business card. "I'm Detective Vasquez."

"Sure, no problem," she said, taking the card. For a moment, she saw Detective Vasquez look past her into her home, doing a quick scan. She interrupted his probing eyes. "Is there anything else I can help you with?"

He returned his focus to her. "No, that's it for now. Thanks again."

She went back inside and closed and locked the door. After

throwing the business card in her purse, out of sight, she decided to open a new bottle of wine. Maybe a rosé this time, since it was such a nice day.

She changed out of her pajamas and threw on a breezy yellow sundress, then walked into her backyard, full glass of chilled rosé in hand, settling onto her back porch steps. As she took her first sip, she noticed her hand was shaking.

She worked her way to the bottom of her wine glass and became introspective, trying to unearth the real reason she hadn't reported the kidnapping, and the real reason she'd lied to that detective. If she were being honest with herself, this wasn't new behavior. It was the same reason she'd happily been an accomplice to her high school boyfriend stealing a car when they were teenagers and had reveled in the thrill of their grand theft auto joyride adventure. It was the same reason she'd tried all the recreational drugs during her college trip to Ibiza and had let a group of three hot Spanish men run a train on her during a rave. It was the same reason she'd smuggled a bag of cocaine through TSA on a flight to San Francisco for New Year's Eve when she was 25. She had a secret passion for danger. That fight-or-flight physical feeling was something she'd always chased. She loved the adrenaline. Some people found it by jumping out of planes. She found it through committing victimless crimes. Sure, she was a boring housewife now, but she hadn't always been that way. She'd been fun. She'd been edgy. She'd been dangerous. She'd just lost sight of that over the years as she grew up and her career took off and she settled down with Craig. But Craig dragging her away from her sense of purpose had somehow reawakened that insatiable urge inside of her to live life on the edge. She craved danger.

After refilling her glass and tiring of scrolling through her

18

Instagram feed on her phone, she left her perch and ventured out to explore the rest of her backyard, inspecting the orange trees toward the back of the property. She thought about how the lush yard would make a nice watercolor and made a mental note to paint it soon. But every few seconds, she'd impulsively glance over at her neighbors' backyard. At the shed. Dead or alive, there was a man locked in that shed. People were looking for him. The police were looking for him. She had just lied to a police detective. What was this dangerous game she was playing? She continued to stare at the shed.

"Needs a little work."

The abrupt voice startled her, sloshing wine out of her glass. She turned around and saw Hayden standing on the other side of the fence, watching her look into his backyard.

"I'm sorry, what?"

"The shed. It needs some work. I've been meaning to repaint it for a while. Maybe even turn it into an outdoor refrigerator."

Like for keeping dead bodies? The thought flew through her mind.

"Oh, sorry I wasn't trying to creep on your backyard. I was just checking out my orange trees," she said, feeling her face get hot.

Hayden laughed, which made his dimples even more defined. "All good. Creep all you want." He ran his hands through his greasy, long hair as his eyes moved down her body, doing a subtle but noticeable checkout. "What did you say your name was again? I didn't catch it the first time since your husband spoke for you."

"Hey!" she fired back. "My husband does *not* speak for me. I'm Blake. And you're...Hayden?" She pretended like she hadn't been saying that name over and over in her head for the past 24 hours.

"Yes." He walked closer toward the fence, his unbreaking eye contact becoming uncomfortable again. She looked away.

"Sorry I made you spill your wine." He eyed her now empty glass.

"Maybe that second glass wasn't meant to be," she joked. "I should probably get back to unpacking..." She looked down at her empty glass awkwardly, afraid to maintain the intense eye contact.

"I know you saw us yesterday," Hayden said. She looked up to meet his eyes. They were serious now, threatening.

"I don't know what you m—"

"Don't play dumb. It's not a good look for you. I can tell you're a smart woman, which was made clear when you didn't say anything to that cop earlier."

"How do you even know..."

"It doesn't matter. What matters is that I can trust you. If we're going to be neighbors, it's important that we can trust each other. Do you understand?"

"I think so." She was sure he could hear how loud her heart was beating.

"Did you tell your husband what you saw?

"He doesn't need to worry."

"Good girl."

She stood there awkwardly, not knowing what to say next.

"Enjoy the rest of your afternoon," he said, starting to walk away from her. "Oh, and Blake."

"Yeah?" Hearing her name come from his mouth sent tingles down her inner thighs.

"That dress looks good on you." He opened the door to the side entrance of his house and went inside before she could respond.

She stood there paralyzed for a moment. She was entering into dangerous territory.

Later that evening, she bought groceries to cook dinner, despite Craig's comments that morning. She figured she could just leave him leftovers in the fridge, which he could reheat when he finally came home. And she was bored and needed a task. *Next step is to find a yoga studio and find hobbies to fill my time. I can't sit around at home all day every day.*

As she sat down at her kitchen table to eat the pasta dish she'd created, she heard loud voices and music coming from next door. Unable to restrain herself, she walked over to the window and opened the curtain. Next door, there were at least a dozen motorcycles parked in the driveway, and two young women were standing on the front steps smoking cigarettes, beers in hand. From this distance, they looked maybe early 20s, both beautiful, thin, with large (probably) fake boobs, and both in shorts that exposed the bottom of their butt cheeks, paired with platform heels. One of them had a giant snake tattoo running down her outer right thigh. *Classy.*

Red opened the front door, amplifying the loud music coming from inside.

"Ladies," he slurred, wobbling on his feet, and sliding his arms around their shoulders. "Who wants to do shots? I've got 'em lined up inside."

The girls shrugged and put their cigarettes out in the lawn, stomping the butts with their heels and following Red back into the house.

Guess they're having a party. I wonder if Hayden is participating...

She wandered out to her back porch, leaving her untouched

dinner on the table, and peered from behind her new hiding spot: the wooden beam that supported the awning above. Scanning the house, she saw a light on in one of the upstairs bedrooms. Two figures appeared in the window, locked in an embrace. As they shifted around, she realized it was Hayden and some woman with long, dark hair. They were passionately kissing. As she watched him hungrily take off the woman's top, she felt a pang of jealousy.

Stop it, Blake. You're married.

Snapping back to reality, she pried her eyes away from the intimate scene in the window and was about to sneak back inside her house when she heard the neighbors' back door open. Three bikers piled out into the backyard, joking loudly with each other, clearly intoxicated. It was too dark in the backyard to make out their faces, but she could see they were all wearing the matching vests.

"Come on, man. You can at least give him real food. He's a human being," one of the men said through laughter.

Another man who appeared to be carrying a bowl of something was walking toward the shed in the back corner of the yard and retorted, "He's a dog. He deserves dog food."

The third man joined in behind the man with the bowl of dog food and chimed in. "He's lucky we're even feeding him at all, disgusting piece of shit that he is. We should probably get in a few more punches in case he's healing from yesterday. We don't want him feeling like he's on vacation at a bed and breakfast."

All three men walked into the shed and shut the door behind them.

She didn't want to stick around to see how long they'd be in there. But at least now she knew the man in the shed was alive.

She glanced back to the upstairs window, but the light was off now. *They're probably having sex.* She went back inside to eat her dinner.

Around midnight, she awoke to the sound of the front door being unlocked and opening. *Craig must be home.* When he didn't come into the bedroom after several minutes, she got up to see where he was. The guest bathroom door was closed, and the shower was running.

"Craig?" she called through the door.

"Hey, honey!" Craig called back. "I went for a run after work, so I thought you'd appreciate me getting clean before getting in bed. Didn't want to wake you up by using our master bath shower."

She opened the bathroom door and peered in. His running shorts and hoodie were on the floor.

"I can't believe they're making you work such long hours," she said, softer now that she was in the bathroom with him. *He gambles.* The fleeting thought raced through her mind before she shook it off, willing herself to believe him.

He poked his head around the shower curtain, shampoo dripping down his forehead. "Well, the company's finances are a mess, and they need me to come in and fix everything to get them ready to go public. You know that's why Bill poached me and brought me in as a consultant."

"I get it," she said, yawning.

His expression softened when he saw his sleepy wife standing there, implying she wanted him around more. "Don't worry, it won't be like this forever. Just for the next couple of months until I can get them in a better place. That's what they've hired me to do."

"Alright, I'm going back to bed."

"See you in there for a snuggle in a minute," he said as he shut the curtain and returned to showering. She was asleep before he got into bed.

The next morning, she was surprised to see Craig still in bed next to her when she awoke. She glanced at her phone on the bedside table. 8 a.m.

"Craig," she said, gently shaking his shoulder to wake him up. "Don't you need to be up for work?"

"It's Saturday, babe."

This was news to her. She'd completely lost track of the days, not having a job to keep her in a routine.

"Listen, I was thinking maybe we could go to the beach today and take a nice, long walk together," Craig said, rolling over to face her in bed. "You've been working so hard on the house; you deserve a little sunshine and fun."

She felt the guilt rising inside her for everything that had transpired the past few days. She'd never really kept secrets from him before, but for some reason she felt like she couldn't share what was going on next door. Perhaps it had something to do with her own participation in the events and feeling like it would be too hard to explain. She was ashamed of witnessing a violent crime and not reporting it, and even more ashamed of fantasizing about her gangster next-door neighbor. Maybe it would be good for her to spend time with her husband.

"Sure," she finally said. "Sounds like fun."

They pulled onto the main road that connected their neighborhood to the beachfront part of Ventura, driving along the humble rows of Mexican markets and thrift shops. Everything had a very flat, single-story aesthetic and the street names were mostly luxurious-sounding Spanish words and phrases. Once they passed the train tracks and drove into the nicer area, the buildings became more and more manicured with every block that led toward the beach. They parked near the boardwalk and strolled along the beautiful ocean-adjacent path, amid teenagers riding beach cruisers and couples perched on the romantic lookout benches. The consistent light breeze throughout the boardwalk made the palm trees sway back and forth, like a dance. Ventura was truly a beautiful place, with its small town but still urban feel.

After spending the afternoon at the beach, she and Craig had dinner at a local beachside café before returning home for the evening. To her pleasant surprise, they had a nice day together, with very few passive-aggressive exchanges. Maybe they were starting to get back into a better rhythm again. Maybe everything could work out for them.

But there was also the man in the shed next door. And the neighbor she lusted after who was keeping that man as a prisoner. Sooner or later, she'd have to navigate how to deal with all of that. Could she and Craig really have a fresh start and be true life partners if she kept this dark secret from him?

Chapter 3

As the weeks passed, she was finally getting in the groove of her new life. She'd set up an art studio in their spare bedroom and was chipping away at a series of oceanic landscapes. She'd joined a yoga studio and had implemented daily morning runs along the beach. She did her best to fill her days with healthy, productive things, trying to make the best of her newfound "freedom" from the burden of having a job.

But every day, she still found herself spying on her fascinating neighbors, watching the man-in-the-shed song and dance become routine: short-lived moral argument among the captors, followed by feeding of the prisoner, followed by (what she assumed was) physical abuse of the prisoner. Then most nights they had parties or small get-togethers, and there would be several additional motorcycles parked in the driveway, different scantily clad women scattered about the property, beer bottles being thrown all over, cigarette butts smashed all over the sidewalks out front.

"I'm really considering saying something to them about all that garbage left out front every day," Craig said to her one day. "I know there's no HOA here, but it's really rude to leave cigarette butts in common areas like the sidewalks."

"I think it's best to just leave it," she'd said, nervous that her husband would do something stupid and piss off the potentially dangerous neighbors. "I can sweep out front when I do my routine housekeeping. It's no big deal."

Fortunately, that seemed to suffice for Craig, for now. "I still don't like it though..."

The dichotomy between her new life in Ventura and her old one in Phoenix was often so jarring that she felt like she'd literally lived two different lives. Phoenix Blake had been ambitious, social, relatively normal. Phoenix Blake had been surrounded by educated, like-minded, productive members of society. Conversely, Ventura Blake was a bored housewife hungry for adventure. Ventura Blake was surrounded by criminals and people hiding secrets, a reality that could be dangerous for her. She found it hard to reconcile her two worlds, her two lives. But the adrenaline junkie inside of her had always been there; it had just been buried for years beneath routine and purpose.

She was becoming obsessed with the neighbors. Obsessed with the man in the shed. She spent a good chunk of her days imagining what the man in the shed looked like, who he was, what he did to end up as a prisoner. She fantasized for weeks about the secret life of Hayden and his friends and what went on behind the scenes, what deeper, darker world lay buried beneath the façade of harmless party boys with motorcycles. She was lost in thought about this one day as she walked along the Ventura Pier, the cool, wet sea breeze blowing through her hair, offsetting the warmth of the direct sun on her skin. As she reached the edge of the long pier, she looked out into the vast ocean. Her life seemed small in comparison to this endless ocean. Her world had changed so much in such a short amount of time, moving from a fully established social and professional life to this strange, new isolated life by the sea.

A hoard of motorcycles roared in the distance behind her, interrupting her thoughts. She turned to face the beach and the road behind it, which appeared tiny in front of the vast mountains surrounding it, but the motorcycles had already passed. She wondered if it was Hayden or his friends. Wandering back down the pier toward the beach parking lot, she tried to push her newfound obsessions from her thoughts and force herself into the present, into her new life. *I need to make good choices.* She sighed. *Easier said than done.*

On a particularly beautiful day while Craig was at work, she decided to break out her outdoor lounger and sunbathe in the backyard. Shimmying into her skimpiest black bikini for the least number of tan lines, she headed outside with sunscreen and a book. She climbed into her lounger, popped in her earbuds, and hit play on Spotify. Sliding her sunglasses from the top of her head to cover her eyes, she let the sun warm her body.

After a while she opened her eyes again, ready to open up her book, when she saw movement out of the corner of her eye. She glanced to her right and saw Hayden walking in his side yard through the hole in the fence. He was talking to someone on the phone and pacing back and forth. She hit pause on her music to eavesdrop.

"—No, man. I fucking told you already. He needs to pay today. We've already given him more time. It's not my fault he has a gambling problem. Tell him to stop hanging around with that fucking Hector and get his shit together. No more excuses. It's today, or there will be consequences."

He hung up with such force that she could practically hear the end call button from across the yard. She turned her face away from him, trying to make it look like she didn't know he was there. The anger in his voice had scared her. Was he in charge? And were people afraid of him? What was he going to do to this mystery person if they didn't pay him? What kind of business was he in? Was this somehow related to the man in the shed? She had so many questions.

Out of the corner of her eye, she saw him notice her and stop pacing. As she felt his eyes on her, she didn't want him to stop looking. It was one thing when they were face-to-face, and she couldn't engage his intensity without revealing her obvious desire. But now, with him watching her, and him not knowing she knew he was watching her...it felt...different. Her fear of him combined with the excitement of the danger he brought into her life turned her on. *Maybe I should put on a little show.*

She reached to the ground for her sunscreen, applied a generous amount into her hands, and sensually massaged it into her arms and legs, conscious of every movement, making it look as sexy as possible. She could still see him out of her peripheral vision, but she didn't dare look his way. She didn't want this little peepshow to end. When the lotion was all rubbed in, she needed a new task to keep him interested. *I know.* She tried not to smile deviously as she reached her hands to the back of her neck, arching her back as she did it, untying the strings of her bikini top. Carefully holding the bathing suit in place so her breasts weren't exposed, she tucked the ties underneath her, trying to tantalize him with her barely covered body. Finally, she ran out of sexy things to do, so she just laid there, wondering how long he would stand there watching.

She heard him clear his throat loudly. Turning to face him, she held her bikini top in place to keep her nipples from popping out.

"What's up, Mrs. Davis?" His tone was playful, a complete 180 from the way he'd just been talking on his phone.

She pretended to pause her already paused music, and said, "Ha, I'd reciprocate the formality, but I don't know your last name."

"Why don't you come over for a drink, and I can show you my whole family tree."

She bit her lip. "Umm, I can't right now. Sorry."

"Yeah, you look pretty busy," he teased.

"No, it's not that. I just don't know if that's...appropriate?"

"Well obviously I would expect you to put some clothes on before you come over. I wouldn't recommend you be half naked in this house full of thirsty men."

They both laughed. "Rain check?" she asked, a little more flirtation in her voice than she intended.

"Sure," he replied, very clearly eyeing her exposed body. After a moment he continued, "I hope our little get-togethers haven't been keeping you and the hubs up at night."

"Not at all," she lied. "Although, we wouldn't mind if you guys picked up all those cigarette butts in the driveway and sidewalk the morning after."

He laughed at this. "I like your balls, girl. I'll see what we can do about the cigarettes." Then, outlining the giant hole in the fence with his hands, added, "And maybe about this hole too. Although I have to say I'm kind of liking the view."

She blushed and prayed he couldn't see.

"See you around, Mrs. Davis."

At 8 p.m., Craig still wasn't home. He'd finally sent a text at 7:30 p.m. with a series of emojis: a skull, a shovel, and a crying face, with the caption, "They're digging me into an early grave. Send help! Be home late—don't wait up. Promise to make it up to you this weekend. Xoxo."

The text sent her reeling into anger. She was instantly transported back in time to when she'd been promoted to a director position, which came with both better pay and much more grueling hours and responsibilities. Craig had praised her at first, taking her out to celebrate her success and bragging about her to his friends. But as the weeks and months wore on and her hours extended later and later, he became resentful. Every time she'd have to travel to meet a client, he'd make her feel guilty, like she was neglecting him as a husband. After six months of her new position taking a toll on their relationship, she requested a meeting with her boss to discuss her role at the company. During an honest conversation about work-life balance, they found a solution where she could maintain her title but have her direct report—a junior staffer—do most of the traveling on her behalf. The compromise seemed to work well for the first few months. Blake was coming home at a regular time and not traveling so much on the weekends, and Craig was warming back up to her. It shouldn't have come as a surprise, though, that when the next round of organizational changes occurred within the company, her direct report was promoted over her for an exciting celebrity-facing position. She'd never forget the day she found out about the promotion. She'd been so angry at Craig that she'd rallied Jasmine to go out for drinks after work and proceeded to get borderline blacked-out on tequila shots. In the morning, Craig was cold to her again, giving her a hard time for getting so drunk. It was impossible to win with him.

And now it was her turn to watch her husband enjoy his success, which also came with long and grueling hours, and she'd been trying her hardest to be supportive. She didn't want to be a hypocrite and was determined not to behave the way he had when it was her time to shine. So instead, she just sulked on the inside, harboring her resentment inside their new life in Ventura.

She'd never showered after lying in the sun and was still walking around the house in her bikini, sipping on a glass of wine. Deciding to call it an early night, she began her routine of locking up the house before getting into a nice, hot bath. But as she passed the kitchen window facing the neighbors' house to close the curtain, something caught her eye on the second story. The light was on in the same bedroom where she'd seen Hayden having a hot make-out session with the mysterious dark-haired girl. She was just about to close the curtain when Hayden appeared in the window. He was naked with a towel wrapped around his waist, clearly fresh out of the shower. She squinted her eyes to get a better look and took in the beauty of his body. His arms were muscular, but not overly jacked, and his abs were contoured into perfection, forming an inviting V shape moving down to the top of the towel. As she let her gaze linger, he suddenly noticed her and looked directly at her. There was no hiding now. She'd been caught looking. He smiled down at her and nodded his head as if to say, "What's up?" She waved back awkwardly.

They both stood there in their respective windows, him in a towel and her in her bikini, for a moment longer than would have been appropriate. After a few seconds, he did the unthinkable. *Maybe even more unthinkable than kidnapping and holding a man prisoner.* He dropped his towel. It was no accident. He faced her head on, looking her in the eyes as he did it. And from what she could see, he liked what he was seeing too.

What the hell do I do? Do I let this go further—like a crazy

person—or do I shut the curtain and go to bed—like a good person?
For a moment she stood there, paralyzed.

And then, impulsively, she set her wine glass down and reached for the back of her neck again, untying her bikini top. This time, she took the entire top off, and dropped it on the floor. He smiled down at her. Then he moved his hand up his body and looked like he was about to stroke himself.

Panic surged inside of her. She threw her arms over her chest and dramatically slammed the curtain shut.

Oh no oh no oh no oh no oh no. This was not good. She ran to the bathroom, skipped the planned hot bath, opting instead for a cold shower to calm herself down, and then went straight to bed.

She was asleep for hours before Craig crawled into bed next to her. When she awoke in the morning, she rolled over to see her husband lying there peacefully, with his back turned to her. Guilt rushed through her and she reached out to lightly stroke her husband's bare back. He rustled a little and turned over to face her.

"OH MY GOD!" she screamed, fully jumping out of bed.

Craig's entire face was black and purple, his lips were swollen to double their normal size, one of his eyes was swollen almost completely shut, and there was caked blood all over his face and hairline.

"Hey, babe," he said through his swollen mouth, immediately recoiling in pain from speaking.

"What the fuck happened?" she screamed back at him.

"Babe, calm down. It's ok," he said carefully without moving his mouth too much. "I was mugged on my way home from work last night."

"Jesus! Did you call the police? Are you ok? Why didn't you

wake me up?"

"It was late, and I knew you'd be asleep. I didn't want to worry you. It was all over so fast. These guys in masks jumped me outside my office building, stole my wallet and watch, beat me up, and then just left. They didn't take my car keys, so I was able to drive home. I just figured I'd deal with it in the morning."

"What if you had a concussion? You should have woken me up," she lectured, running out of the room to retrieve their first aid kit and ice packs. "You stay in bed!" she ordered.

She played nurse most of the morning, after forcing Craig to call in sick to work.

"It's Friday anyway," she'd reasoned. "You can go back on Monday."

She'd suggested they file a police report, but Craig didn't seem to think it would make a difference since he wouldn't be able to I.D. the masked men. He said he just wanted to move on. After all, in his eyes, it was just some credit cards which could easily be replaced, and a watch which, while valuable, was several years old anyway. She felt the familiar suspicion rise inside of her, wondering if this was some conspiracy and if Craig was in trouble, but she reminded herself that Craig had *wanted* to move far away from his gambling problems. Why would he start it up again now in this new place? It wouldn't make sense. *I'm probably just being crazy.*

And the truth was, she was afraid of having the police come to their house. She didn't want to risk that detective—what was it, Vasquez? —coming back. She'd lied to him once but wasn't sure how well she'd fare a second time, especially in this crisis with her husband so badly beaten. And she didn't want Hayden to see police at her house for any reason, even if unrelated to the prisoner in his shed. It was all just too risky at this point. So, she didn't press the issue and instead followed Craig's lead.

Chapter 4

By the following Monday, Craig's face had healed enough to where he could return to work. She went about her daily ritual of practicing morning yoga and spending the afternoon painting. Her art studio was piling up with canvas upon canvas of beach-themed scenery, and while she lacked inspiration, she forced the routine to stay busy. Anything to keep herself from spying on the neighbors or thinking about Hayden, or about the man in the shed.

That afternoon, as she stared at a blank canvas, feeling especially unimaginative, she heard her phone buzzing on the kitchen counter.

"Jasmine!" she screamed into the phone with excitement.

"How's my favorite California housewife doing?" Jasmine teased. Blake was so relieved to hear from someone from her old life. They'd texted here and there, but this was the first time hearing her voice since the move.

"Umm, well you know," Blake said. "Living that *housewife* life. It's a big adjustment. I don't think it's fully sunk in yet, but I already miss working so much."

"Girl, enjoy the time off! You've been working your whole adult life! You deserve some time to just chill."

"Ugh, I guess."

"Just give it a year—you can always get a job out there if you get bored."

"Yeah, you're right," Blake said. "It has been nice having more time to focus on myself. No brag, but I'm getting really tan and fit."

"Well, aren't you just the little yogini! How are things with Craig? Have they been better since you finally made the move?"

"Things have been mostly fine," she said casually before remembering she had big news. "Umm except he was mugged the other night—right outside his office! These guys in masks jumped him and he came home looking like he'd been in a car accident. It was so scary."

She couldn't tell Jasmine about the underlying suspicions she'd been having about the mugging. She'd never divulged Craig's past gambling issues to her best friend because she didn't have the energy for the inevitable judgment. She'd kept it a secret and made the tough decision to handle it on her own with her husband.

"Holy shit! I thought Ventura is supposed to be safe! Is he ok?"

"Yeah, he's fine. His office is in a part of town that can be a little sketchier in some places. We spent the past few days staying super lowkey until his face healed, but he went back to work today. He even let me put a little concealer around his eyes this morning where there was still some bruising."

"Aww, the pretty princess," Jasmine joked.

"Speaking of which," Blake said. "I just realized I never washed the clothes he came home in that night. They were totally covered in blood. I should go find them and see if they're salvageable."

"Always the good wife."

"Actually...I haven't been a very good wife recently," Blake confessed.

"What, you forgot to fold his laundry or something?"

"No, bitch," Blake shot back playfully. "Like, I've kind of been flirting with our next-door neighbor."

"Ohhh, bad girl! Tell me everything."

"There's not much to tell. He's so not my type. I'm pretty sure he's in, like, a motorcycle club or something," she said, keeping it vague, unsure how much she wanted to reveal.

"You mean like *Sons of Anarchy*? Like Jax??" Jasmine asked excitedly.

"I mean, no one compares to our great love, Charlie Hunnam. But yeah, I don't know if that show is what it's like in real life. I honestly don't know what his deal is or what he does. But he's like, dirty and grungy. And kind of rude."

"Sounds hot," Jasmine said.

"But there's something about him...that's just...sexy."

"Girl, I get it. I'm all about those bad-boy types," Jasmine said. "Also, probably why I'm still single at 35."

The girls laughed.

"Hey, the heart wants what the heart wants," Blake said.

"And the V wants what the V wants too, clearly," Jasmine teased.

Blake desperately missed her best friend. The last time she'd gotten together with Jasmine was two nights before the big move. They'd gone out to their favorite bar in Phoenix and spent most of the night draining vodka sodas and reminiscing on some of their favorite friendship memories. Toward the end of the night when the alcohol lowered their inhibitions and provided lubrication for speaking the truth, things got heavier. Blake admitted how angry she was at Craig for

38

asking her to move to California and shared her fear that their marriage would inevitably fall apart. Despite Jasmine's internal passed judgment, she kept her poker face for the sake of their friendship and remained diplomatic. She mused to Blake that this move would be a good test for their marriage, to see if it could stand the test of time. And if it didn't work out in the end, that would be a good thing to know sooner rather than later.

"Anyway," Blake said, shifting back to the present phone call and changing the subject from Hayden. "What's up with you? How are things at Smith & Hansen? Did Sandy get fired yet? I need all the details!"

"Ooh, girl, I have some serious tea to spill!"

Jasmine filled her in on all the gossip and drama of her former workplace as Blake walked into the master bedroom to rummage through the walk-in closet and retrieve Craig's bloody clothes from the night he was jumped. She put the phone on speaker and set it down on a shelf while Jasmine talked, as she squatted down and dug around in the piles of clothes on the floor. *God, Craig is such a slob.* Finding the bloody shirt and pants, she loaded them into a laundry basket along with some other dirty clothes, when she spotted something strange.

There was a silver object poking out of one of Craig's running shoes. She scooted closer to grab the shoe. As she pulled it toward her, she realized the silver item inside the shoe was a phone. An older iPhone that she didn't recognize.

"...and so, then everyone pretty much shunned Sandy after she said she didn't think mothers should qualify for disability as part of maternity leave. No one invites her to lunch anymore. It's kind of sad."

Blake realized she hadn't been listening to anything Jasmine had been saying.

"Hey! Can I call you back?" she interrupted Jasmine's story.

"Oh, umm, sure. No problem."

"Sorry, something just came up. It was great to hear from you!"

She hung up her phone and pulled the old iPhone out of her husband's shoe, staring at it. *Why would he keep an old phone in a shoe in our closet?*

The phone was off. She held down the "on" button and waited. The Apple icon appeared. After what felt like an eternity, the locked home screen finally showed up.

Six notifications.

Five were from someone named Kendra.

One was from someone named Hector.

What. The. Fuck.

She hit unlock and was prompted to enter a passcode. *Fuck.* She tried a few combinations—his birthday, her birthday. Nothing. After the fifth or sixth try, the low battery warning popped up and the iPhone promptly shut off.

"NO!" she screamed out loud. Looking at the bottom of the phone, she realized it took an older version of the iPhone charger, so she couldn't plug it into hers. *Fucking Apple.*

She remembered that Craig had a plastic bin with spare chargers out in the garage, and ran, dead iPhone in hand, to go see if any of them matched this phone. Once she spotted the bin filled to the brim with tangled wires, she dug through until she found an older iPhone charger with the wider plug-in. She grabbed it and headed back to the kitchen to charge the phone, when she heard Craig's car pull up in the driveway.

"Shit!" she screamed out loud. Frantically, she shoved the charger back into the bin, closed the lid and sprinted to the bedroom to put the phone back in the shoe where she'd found it. Craig opened the door and waltzed into their house just as she emerged from the closet, positive the guilt and adrenaline were apparent on her face.

"Honey, I'm home!" Craig said in his best Ricky Ricardo impression. She cringed. She hated when he did accents.

"What are you doing home so early?" she asked, trying not to sound caught off guard. She glanced at the clock. It was only 4:30 p.m.

"Why does it feel like you're mad at me for coming home at a reasonable time?" He laughed as he set his keys and wallet on the mantle by the door.

"Not at all. Just surprised." She forced a smile. "New wallet?" She eyed the folded black leather.

"Oh yeah," he said. "Went to a shop by work today and picked one up. All my replacement credit and debit cards should be coming in the mail soon too."

"Which reminds me," he said, walking over to her and planting a kiss on her forehead, holding her arms in his hands. "Mind if I use your debit card for a bit until my new one comes in the mail?"

"Sure," she said casually. *But who the hell is Kendra and who the hell is Hector?* "I can just use a credit card if I need to shop."

"Thanks, babe."

"So why are you home early today?"

"I thought you'd never ask!" he said playfully. "Your

41

charmer of a husband just landed the company an amazing fucking offer. We're being acquired!"

"Oh wow," she said, feigning excitement. "I thought the plan was to go public?"

"Only if someone didn't buy us first. This is even better!"

"That's great!" she said, forcing another smile. "Congratulations."

"Bill wants to celebrate tonight, and suggested we bring the wives. Are you up for going to a restaurant in Santa Barbara with Bill and Sarah?"

Before she could respond, he grabbed her by the waist and picked her up in the air, twirling her around like a teenager in love. *A teenager in love...with someone named Kendra. And possibly Hector.*

"Alright, go get ready and we'll go in 45. Yeah?" he called to her as he walked toward their master bath to shower.

Guess I'll have to wait until later to find out what's on that phone.

As they drove up the 101 freeway toward Santa Barbara, Blake took in the incredible view. To the left, the sun was setting over the vast Pacific Ocean, casting a pink and orange glow over the horizon. Despite averaging 70 miles per hour, they drove with the windows down to soak in the cool, misty ocean breeze. The ocean smell reminded her why she'd agreed to move to the beach in the first place. It smelled like freedom.

Once they exited the freeway, they cruised down Cabrillo Boulevard, an endless stretch of beachfront hotels and restaurants in Santa Barbara, lined with thousands of perfectly aligned rows of palm trees. It was the quintessential California coastline. Pulling into the hotel valet at the restaurant where they'd planned to meet Bill and Sarah, Blake felt anxious. She couldn't get her mind off the secret phone and the mystery people in it and didn't know how she'd successfully get through this social event with her husband's boss and his wife, pretending to be a happy housewife.

"Craig!" a man's voice called from the bar. Bill. Craig and Blake waved back and walked to meet the couple. "I ordered a bottle of wine with four glasses. Hope you both like Merlot?"

You literally couldn't have picked a worse red wine.

"Sounds great." Blake beamed as the couples made their introductions. Bill was a bit of a silver fox and acted like someone who was previously and potentially currently a playboy. Like the kind of guy who took his wedding ring off on business trips. He had charisma and took charge in group settings, ordering for everyone and playing host. She'd met him a couple of times, but this was her first social outing with him.

Sarah, on the other hand, was milder and more aloof. Both her personality and outfit were reserved: her pearls and cardigan perfectly matched her uptight demeanor. When Blake had asked her if she worked, Sarah had stated matter-of-factly that it was more important for her to stay home with the kids and be present for their upbringing.

"I don't understand how those career moms do it," she said. "How can you find the time to really connect with your child when you're gone nine hours a day?"

You and Craig would be perfect for each other. When Blake didn't respond, instead taking a long sip of wine at the end of this speech, Sarah continued.

"And when are you two lovebirds planning to have kids?"

It was the age-old question, the question strangers felt was appropriate to ask all married couples. She smiled and politely responded with, "Someday, when the time is right," before changing the topic of conversation.

Blake zoned out while Craig and Bill talked shop, and Sarah rambled on in a sidebar conversation about the rising homelessness problem in their beautiful town of Santa Barbara.

"Well, if I were homeless, I'd live here too," Blake said. "The weather is perfect all year long, so there's no harsh winter to brave. And your 'bedroom' has breathtaking ocean views on one side and striking mountain views on the other. You can't really beat that."

Sarah raised an eyebrow at this and returned her focus to her wine. When the bill finally came, Blake was ecstatic to escape the uncomfortable situation.

After their expensive dinner, they drove the 30-mile stretch home and climbed into bed. And when Craig tried to put the moves on her, she feigned an upset stomach. "Sorry, babe. Not tonight."

It took her forever to fall asleep. Her mind was racing, thinking about what was on that mystery phone. And the neighbors were having another party next door, music blaring. She imagined Hayden was having sex with the dark-haired girl again. Or maybe a new girl tonight. She wondered if any of those girls knew there was a prisoner in the backyard shed, or if it was a secret among the bikers.

Finally, her Xanax kicked in (she secretly took some when Craig wasn't looking—he didn't like her using it for sleep), and she fell into a deep slumber. All night, she had vivid Xanax dreams involving Hayden, her riding on the back of his bike as their hair blew in the wind and she cozied her arms around his chest, hugging him tight.

In the morning, she awoke to Craig's daily kiss on the forehead. Slowly coming back to reality, she remembered everything from the day before. The phone. The secret.

She waited for him to leave and lock the door behind him before she jumped out of bed to retrieve the iPhone from the closet and the charger from the garage. But when she plugged in the charger to the phone and turned it on, she saw that it had a full battery.

Her hands were shaking again. If the battery was full, that meant that Craig had charged it at some point between the time he came home yesterday and when he left for work that morning—which meant he checked it after they went to bed.

Did Craig get up while I was sleeping to go plug in his fucking burner phone?

She stared at the locked home screen. No new notifications. She tried several more passcodes, trying to think of every meaningful series of numbers she could, and was starting to worry she'd get locked out of the phone for 24 hours if she didn't guess it soon. In a desperate attempt to try everything, she entered 696969. The phone unlocked. *That motherfucker.*

Taking a deep breath, she opened his text messages. The only contacts were Kendra and Hector. She started with Kendra.

Her plan was to scroll to the beginning of their chat and start there, but the latest exchange paralyzed her.

> *Kendra: When are you going to cum over so I can sit on your face? {sent at 10 a.m. Sunday}*
>
> *Craig: Wednesday babe. Just need to come up with a 'working-late' excuse so I can cum see you. Miss that body of yours. {sent at 3 a.m. Tuesday morning}*

She gagged when she saw that they'd both spelled *come* as *cum*. And he'd opened his phone in the middle of the night while she was sleeping to send that message. She felt stomach bile rising inside of her and ran to the bathroom to vomit. After several minutes of dry heaving, she wiped her face and went back to look through the phone.

So, Craig is having an affair. She let the words surface in her brain, now that the nausea had passed. Closing her eyes, she flicked her index finger upwards, scrolling to the top of the conversation as fast as she could. When she reached the beginning, she saw the date of their first exchange. It was two months before she and Craig had moved there, which meant that the affair started when he was routinely flying out to California to "start his job early and get the house in order."

That pig.

Next, she braved herself to open the chat with Hector. *Is he having an affair with this Hector, too?* She wasn't sure she could handle Craig being secretly bisexual on top of being unfaithful. She opened the Hector chat. There were only 5 messages total—she didn't even need to scroll to see the entire conversation.

Hector: You have until Thursday to pay up. {sent the previous Monday}

Craig: I'm good for it. I'll have the money to you by then. {sent that same Monday}

Hector: I'm not fucking around. Don't play with fire. You have one more day. {sent Wednesday}

Craig: Hey man, my paycheck is coming Friday. Any chance I can have one more day to get you your money?

{sent Wednesday}

Hector: Time's up {sent Thursday}

Her head was spinning as she reread the text chain several times. Thursday...that was the night Craig got mugged.

I fucking knew it.

Craig was gambling again. He owed money. But how? And what serious mess had he gotten himself into? From the sound of these texts, this Hector didn't seem like a bookie. He sounded like...a gangster. Could this be the same Hector that Hayden mentioned on his phone call?

She picked up her own phone and logged into the mobile banking app for their joint account. The amount in their checking and savings looked normal. Did he have a secret account somewhere? Maybe he'd learned from his previous mistakes and gotten better at lying.

She wandered, lightheaded, into the kitchen and opened a bottle of wine. As she popped the cork open, she looked at the clock. 11 a.m.

Chapter 5

When she poured the last glass of Cabernet left in the bottle, she ventured out into the backyard, with the false pretense of picking oranges, and the real intention of spying on the neighbors. *I wonder what Hayden is up to.*

From her yard, she peered through the giant hole and saw that everything looked business as usual. Glancing out front, she saw three motorcycles, and as she scanned the rest of the large house, things appeared to be quiet at the Army of Outlaws house.

Craig is cheating on me. The thought invaded her mind, unwelcome. *Craig is cheating on me and he owes someone named Hector money. Hector is dangerous.*

She shivered off the ugly facts and took another sip of her wine. *I wonder what Hayden looks like naked up-close.* Another unwelcome thought. And as the wine continued to do its job in relieving her of her inhibitions, she got an idea.

She was going to have sex with Hayden.

Feeling wicked, she ran back into the house to shower, shave, and primp. After an hour of moisturizing, smokey-eyeing, and hair curling, she slipped into her faux leather leggings that made her butt look amazing, a low-cut top, and heeled booties.

She brushed the wine residue off her teeth and rinsed with

mouthwash to erase the day's indulgences.

Exhilarated, she walked next door around 6 p.m., ready to play the seduction game. As she clambered through the obstacle-filled front yard for the first time, she noticed the cigarette butts and trash weren't limited to the sidewalks. The whole yard was littered with garbage...and was that...a blood stain in the driveway?

Her liquid courage propelled her forward, and she knocked on the large, blue front door.

A few seconds later, a man's voice responded.

"That you, neighbor?" Not Hayden's voice.

"Yes, it's Blake from next door," she called back.

The door opened, and Red stood there, shirtless and in baggy, grey sweatpants with stains on them. His ribcage was poking through his pale, skinny torso, and he had a tattoo on his left pec of the cowboy skull and crossbones from their vests. He looked stoned.

"It *is* our neighbor!" He turned around to face the room behind him. "Our hot neighbor is here, and she's dressed to the nines."

She was already regretting this decision. But if she could just get to Hayden, then maybe it would all be worth it. Three men came to the door—Elvis, Dave, and someone she didn't recognize. An older man with a long, grizzly beard, pitted acne scars, and a shiny, bald head. No Hayden.

"Damn, girl!" Elvis said emphatically, pantomiming an outline of her curves with his hand. "What can we do for you on this hot day?"

"I was just on my way out to a dinner," she lied. "But I wanted to stop by because Hayden promised to loan me a book."

All three men burst into laughter.

"Hayden...reading??" Red clutched his nonexistent belly in overexaggerated amusement. "I've never seen that guy even get through a birthday card, let alone an entire book."

"What was this book he so sweetly promised to loan you?" Dave asked.

She panicked. "It was a book about motorcycle clubs."

All three men stopped laughing.

"Excuse me?" the unknown bald man said abruptly. He turned to his friends. "What does this bitch think she means?"

Red suddenly looked nervous. "It's all good, Rocco. This is our next-door neighbor, Blake. She's good people."

"We don't know that yet," Dave shot back.

"Guys, I'm totally kidding," Blake said, adrenaline running high. The look on all three of their faces sobered her up, and she was suddenly afraid. They were a lot scarier up close than when she talked to them through their fence. "The truth is... I came here looking for Hayden...not for a book." She motioned to her outfit.

"Ohhh," Red said, breaking into laughter again. "Our girl is hot for El Jefe! Figures." He sighed. "What else is new."

All three laughed, even the third one, Rocco, who was a more intense caliber of intimidating, compared to her young neighbors.

"If only they knew how unhygienic that guy is. I don't think I've ever seen him shower," Dave said. "And yet, they all wanna jump his bones."

"Yeah, we should start throwing parties when he's not here. Might give us more of a fighting chance," Red shot back. He turned back to Blake. "Want to come over tonight, lady?"

"Oh. Does that mean Hayden isn't here?" she said, trying to hide the disappointment in her voice.

"I see how it is," he teased. "Yeah, no. Hayden's on a ride."

"Do you know when he'll be back?" She tried to sound as casual as possible.

Red shrugged his shoulders. "Dunno. Last time he went on a ride it was a few days before he got back."

She backed away. "Ok, well, thanks anyway."

"Honey, you can still come inside and hang with us," Dave said, eyeing her leather leggings.

"No, that's ok, thanks though." She backed away slowly as she said this. Rocco stared at her with disdain, like she'd trespassed on his property and he was ready to attack.

While Rocco stayed silent, Red and Dave jokingly catcalled her as she walked briskly in her heeled boots back up her own driveway and into her own house. *What the hell was I thinking?*

She washed off all her makeup and changed into pajamas. And for the first time since she quit her job and moved, she cried her eyes out.

Chapter 6

When she awoke Wednesday morning, everything she'd learned the day before came crashing back into her mind. Her stomach was twisted, and her chest felt tight. When Craig kissed her forehead goodbye, she pretended to be asleep. She wasn't ready to look him in the eye, and she didn't know yet whether she was going to confront him about the burner phone. There was so much to process, and she needed a plan.

Dragging herself out of bed to shower and get ready for the day, she came up with an idea. She was going to follow Craig that evening. His last text to Kendra had promised a meetup Wednesday night, and today was the day. She wanted to know what this woman looked like, the woman who was wrecking her home.

Throwing open the doors to her walk-in closet, she crouched down to pull out the shoe with the hidden phone, but when she looked inside, there was no phone. *Shit. He must have moved the hiding spot. Or...he has it with him so he can meet up with Kendra tonight.* She'd have to go to Craig's office and wait for him to leave and try to follow him that way. She had no idea where Kendra lived or where they were going to meet up. Why didn't she read through those texts more thoroughly and write down pertinent information? *Oh, yeah, because I was too busy puking my brains out.*

At 4 p.m., she walked out to her black Mazda3 in the driveway, wearing a black hoodie, her biggest sunglasses, and black pants. As she opened the driver's side door, she glanced over to the neighbors' house. Still no sign of Hayden. She got in and started the engine. Once she arrived at Craig's office building and spotted his car, she pulled into a spot about eight spaces over, positioned behind a large, white catering van. It was the perfect spot—she had an unobstructed view of his car, but he wouldn't be able to see her when he came out.

She waited. And waited. 6:30 p.m. rolled around, and he still hadn't left the building. Maybe he really did work late some of these nights.

Her phone buzzed loudly on the center console, making her jump out of her seat. *Jesus.* She picked up the phone to check her text messages.

> *Craig: Hey babe working late tonight (what else is new) {money bag emoji}. I should be home by 11 or 12 but don't wait up. Love you.*

Even though she was expecting a text like this, it still hurt. Craig had been in her life for seven years now, and the first few had been great. *How did everything get so fucked up in such a short amount of time? Why did we start lying to each other and keeping secrets?*

She looked up from her phone to see the lights blink on Craig's Audi. He was walking through the parking lot toward the car. *This is it.* As he climbed inside and turned on the engine, she held her breath and waited for the right moment. Craig pulled out of his parking spot and headed toward the exit. She turned on her car and followed him out of the lot, careful to stay far enough behind that he wouldn't see her, but close enough that she wouldn't lose him at a stoplight.

She continued following him for 10 minutes, driving onto the freeway and into a different part of town that she didn't recognize. Finally, he pulled into a residential neighborhood, and she slowed her own car down to stay off his radar. As he pulled into a dead-end street, she held back for a moment until she saw him park his car. He got out, closing the door quietly, and walked up a well-lit driveway toward a white duplex. She parked her car on the adjacent street, and tiptoed in the shadows toward him, hurrying to get as close to the duplex as possible. Hiding behind a tree next door, she'd found the perfect spot where she was hidden by the darkness but could still see and hear her husband's shoes on the pavement. He knocked on the door and stood there in the flooded front lighting for several seconds, looking down at his hands and picking at his fingernails.

Finally, the door opened, and a woman—presumably Kendra—emerged. From what Blake could see, Kendra had dark hair, the top half piled in a topknot bun, the bottom half sprawled down her shoulders and chest.

"You're 45 minutes late," Kendra said, crossing her arms over her almost bare chest. She was wearing a cropped tank top that exposed most of her large breasts and obnoxiously tiny waist.

"I got held up at work," Craig said. His voice sounded different than when he talked to her, his wife. Much more playful.

"I didn't see you at any meetings this week." Kendra sounded suspicious, as if she were the one being betrayed by Craig.

"Let me in and I'll make it up to you?"

Blake saw a smile spread across the woman's face as she uncrossed her arms and took Craig's hands in hers.

"Alright fine," she said coyly. "But only if you do that thing to me that I like."

"Anything for you," he replied excitedly, and with this answer, the woman pulled him by the necktie into her home and closed the door.

Blake stood there, hiding in the shadows behind the tree for several minutes after the door closed. Finally, after what seemed like hours, she walked weakly back to her car to return home.

As she drove, she rolled the windows all the way down and didn't turn on the radio. She just wanted the loud, warm wind crashing on her skin. She was enraged but also flooded with adrenaline. In her manic state, she almost missed the turn for her neighborhood, and had to slam on the brakes at the last second, nearly hitting the curb. She needed a drink.

When she entered her house and turned on all the lights, she peeked out the kitchen window to check out next door. No lights on in any of the rooms. Complete silence. *Hayden, where are you?*

In a haze, she walked over to the liquor cabinet and grabbed a bottle of vodka. Pouring a generous amount into a glass, she went to the ice maker and filled the remaining space with ice. She wanted to drown in her vodka and numb the pain of knowing her husband was currently fucking another woman. *Another woman he met at a fucking gambling addicts meeting.*

She was in bed but still awake when Craig quietly unlocked the front door. She looked at the clock. 1:30 a.m. *He's not even trying that hard to hide his affair.* She heard him tiptoe into the guest bathroom and turn on the shower. *Showering off the dirty extramarital sex before getting into bed with his wife.*

As she listened to the distant sound of hot water erasing her husband's indiscretion, she thought more about her own secrets and lies. Yes, she'd stopped the window strip tease just in time before it went too far, but what about the night before when she found the secret phone, and she'd knocked on the neighbors' door with the intent of having sex with Hayden? Was she just as guilty as Craig? Were they both at fault? She remembered something Jasmine had told her once about breakups: they were never one sided. Usually, both partners played a role in the demise of their relationship. She wondered how much that applied to her current situation. Her head was spinning from the stiff vodka drink, and she forced herself to stop thinking for the night. When Craig finally turned off the shower and climbed into bed, she pretended to be asleep.

A brutal hangover woke her up, and she was immediately offended by the bright light shining through their bedroom window. Craig was rummaging around in their closet.

"What are you doing?" she asked angrily.

"Oh, sorry for waking you babe," he said, poking his head out from the closet. "I was trying to wait for you to get up before making too much noise, but it's getting late."

She rubbed her temples and sat up in bed to investigate the closet. Craig was packing a small suitcase. When he finally noticed her watching him, he walked over and sat on the bed next to her.

"I have some bad news," he said, rubbing her legs with his hand over the comforter. "I have to go to LA this weekend to meet with the acquisition team. I'm annoyed they asked me to do this so last minute, but these are really important people and I need to be there."

"Ok," she said blankly.

"I'm sorry... I know I haven't been around much lately. Are you mad?"

"It's fine."

"I've been married to you long enough to know that 'it's fine' doesn't mean you're fine. I know you're upset, and you have every right to be," he said, now reaching his hand to her cheek to softly stroke it with his thumb.

She felt her skin burning where he touched it. His touch no longer made her feel safe and warm. It set her on fire. It made her want to set him on fire. She smiled back at him.

"I understand. Business is business," she said, mustering up the strength to provide more than a two-word response. "Go on your trip, it's really fine."

"Thank you for being so wonderful. I promise we will spend more time together next week. After having to work this entire weekend, I'm telling those guys I need to be home by 5 p.m. every night next week to be with my wife!" he declared, shaking his finger playfully in the air. With that, he returned to packing in the closet.

She was relieved. She needed some time apart from him to figure out what her next move was going to be, because she wasn't ready to confront him about what she knew. Maybe this weekend would provide her the space to create a game plan.

"I'll be home on Sunday, ok?" he called to her as he made his way to the front door. "Be good."

Craig and his suitcase then zoomed away in his Audi. She was all alone. For an entire weekend.

Her hangover gave her a specific hankering for fresh-squeezed orange juice, so she threw on jean shorts and a tank top and headed out to the backyard, grabbing a large bowl and a pair of scissors from the kitchen on the way. As the sun beat down on her, she dragged a patio chair over to the tree with the most fruit and climbed barefoot onto it, reaching up high to cut down the juiciest-looking oranges and drop them into her bowl.

"Need some help over there?" a man's voice called to her. Hayden's voice.

As she flipped around to see him, she lost her balance on the chair and sent it flying onto its side, launching her face-first toward the ground. She braced her fall with her hands at the last second, but instantly felt the searing pain of her knees scraping the cement where the grass ended.

"Oh shit!" Hayden yelled from his yard.

Mortified, she tried to quickly jump to her feet, but found they were temporarily paralyzed, still recovering from the fall and not ready to move yet. *Ohmygod, move, you stupid fucking legs!*

She heard a noise at the gate behind her and then suddenly she was being lifted at the waist by strong arms pulling her to her feet.

"I'm so sorry," Hayden said, laughing lightly into her ear from behind her. "I didn't mean to make you fall."

She turned around to face him. His arms were still around her waist, seemingly unaware that they were lingering. She was looking right into Hayden's face, which was just inches from hers. He was even more beautiful this close. His blue eyes had an almost evil quality to them, and his complementary dark features gave him this effortlessly seductive look every time he made eye contact. Which he constantly did.

"Are you ok?" His arms were still around her waist.

"Yeah, I'm fine. That's so embarrassing." She forced a laugh.

"You're bleeding," he noticed, looking down at her knees. She glanced down to where he was looking. Blood was running down her legs from her freshly skinned knees. "Let's get you fixed up."

Without asking permission, Hayden whipped her legs up into his arms and carried her toward her house. As they walked, she braced herself by wrapping her arms around his neck and got a waft of his scent—clean laundry mixed with a hint of body odor.

"Do you have a first aid kit?" he asked.

She nodded. "My husband..."

"Left this morning with a suitcase," he interrupted her, lifting an eyebrow.

"On a business trip," she said.

"Well, is it ok if I come in and bandage you up?"

"Sure." *Danger danger danger.*

Once inside, he lifted her onto the kitchen counter, with her legs dangling down. She gave him instructions to locate the kit in the laundry room, and he came back with the red case in his hands. He was wearing faded jeans with an ornate, over-the-top belt that featured a gaudy gargoyle in its buckle, and a crisp, white V-neck t-shirt, that clung to his muscular, tattooed arms.

"Who's the artist?" he asked abruptly.

"What?"

Hayden gestured to the paintbrushes laying out to dry by the kitchen sink.

"Oh. I guess I am?"

"You're not sure?"

"I paint," she said modestly. "I don't know if I'd consider myself an artist."

"What do you paint?"

"I...have some landscapes and stuff piled up in one of the bedrooms if you want to see. They're nothing to write home about though."

"Mrs. Davis," he smirked, "quit trying to lure me to your bedroom."

"I wasn't—"

"Alright, alright. First thing's first," he said, redirecting the conversation. "We need to disinfect."

He stuck a paper towel under the faucet to wet it and began cleaning up the blood.

"You really don't have to do this. I'm fine," she said.

"Oh, do you want me to go?" he asked, pulling the paper towel back dramatically as if getting ready to leave.

"No," she said, biting her lip.

"That's what I thought." He smiled, returning to cleaning the blood off her knees. She studied the full-sleeve tattoos on both of his arms, which cascaded down onto the backs of his hands. Some designs were interwoven into complicated scenes, and some were standalone pieces. On his left forearm, there was a scene with a mermaid breathing fire onto a pirate ship, which was erupted in the flames.

"I heard you stopped by the other night." He looked up into her eyes, and she felt herself blush.

"Yeah, I umm..." She tried to think of an excuse. Anything. *Say something.* "I wanted to follow up on those cigarette butts that you said you'd pick up. They're still all over the sidewalk."

He smiled. "Normally I think playing coy is annoying, but it's kind of endearing when you do it."

"What does that mean?" she asked, heat rising to her face.

"Ok, if you want to pretend like we didn't see each other

naked..."

He applied rubbing alcohol to her wounds.

"Ow!" she cried out. "I'm not pretending like it didn't happen."

"Good," he said. "Because it was hot. Too bad you closed the curtain before we could find out how that story would have ended."

"I have a feeling I know." She smiled.

"It's cool. You're just the biggest tease ever," he said, his left hand grazing the backs of her legs as his right hand patted the wounds. She was turned on.

"I'm not a tease. I'm married," she said.

"And are you happy?" he asked, a way more direct question than she'd anticipated.

"Marriage is complicated."

"I'm not a bullshit kind of guy. If you want to give bullshit answers, I'm happy to leave you here and let you give them to someone else."

"Things aren't great between us right now."

"Hence the suitcase?"

"No, not 'hence.' I told you it's a business trip."

"Got it," he said, now placing band-aids on her wounds. "Hold still. Your legs keep bouncing around every time you get all worked up."

"Then stop working me up!"

He stood up from his crouched position, his body now wedged in between her legs, their faces close again.

"Alright, I'll stop working you up," he said, leaning in toward her face and sliding his arms around her waist. *Is he going to kiss me? Right here in my kitchen?* Hayden let his face get just millimeters from hers, then lifted her by the waist off the

61

counter and planted her back onto the floor. He backed away from her. "Alright, I'll let you get back to your day then." He moved toward the sliding door.

"You're leaving already?" she asked before she could stop herself.

He turned around, smiling, and looking her up and down. "Yeah. I'm going for a ride."

"Oh."

"Wanna come?"

The invitation caught her by surprise. She bit her lip again, trying to decide.

"If you can't, it's fin—"

"Yes. I want to come."

"Cool." He stared down at her legs again. "Why don't you go put some real clothes on and meet me out front in 15 minutes."

Chapter 7

Thirty minutes later, she emerged from her house. She was sweating from frantically trying to shower, put on makeup, and find a motorcycle-appropriate outfit in such a limited time-frame. Spontaneity was never her strong suit. She'd always been too high maintenance to be one of those #iwokeuplikethis women. But she didn't want Hayden to know that. She wanted to him to see her as easy, low maintenance.

Strutting down her driveway in a pair of high-waisted jeans, black cap-sleeved crop top, combat boots, and a cross-body purse, she felt she'd done well for the short window of time he'd given her. Her hair had even miraculously dried into pretty, long, blonde beach waves that day from the humidity.

Hayden tapped an imaginary watch on his wrist. "You're lucky you look so good. Otherwise, I might be annoyed that you're late."

He was now wearing his leather vest with the skull and wings insignia over his white V-neck.

"Sorry—do you know how hard it is to put jeans on over scraped knees?" She laughed, flirting.

He looked like he was considering this for a second. "Actually, yes." Then he looked at her bare arms. "You're gonna need a jacket. Something warm."

"But it's so hot out," she said, confused.

"It'll be cold by the time we get back."

It was only 3 p.m. How long was he planning to keep her out? She'd come this far without ruining it by asking questions, so there was no point in starting now. She did as she was told and ran inside to grab her vegan leather jacket and re-emerged with it in her arms.

"Ever ridden on the back of one of these?"

"Just once in college. My boyfriend Steve had a Honda but—"

"—So, you've never been on one of *these*." He motioned to his giant Harley Davidson. "Give me your jacket."

She handed him the jacket, and he opened the backseat, stuffing it into the storage below.

"You just need to know three important things before we ride. First, you have to wear the Bitch Helmet. Sorry, it's a rule."

"What's the bitch—"

"—Please hold all questions until the end. Anyway, you wear the Bitch Helmet. Second, your feet go on the pegs back here. And third, you must—and this is the most important one—you need to wrap your arms as tightly around me as you possibly can and don't let go. Understand?"

"Yeah, it's pretty basic..."

"What are the three rules?" he quizzed her, pulling out a black helmet with a skull covered in roses on the back of it, and handing it to her.

"I take it this is the Bitch Helmet?" she asked, taking it in her hands and examining. "I put this thing on my head...and then I put my feet on the pegs and hold you real tight. Did I get it all?"

"A+, College Educated Girl."

Hmm...maybe I shouldn't have mentioned my 'college'

boyfriend.

Hayden put on his own helmet. It was dramatically cooler and sleeker than hers. She eyed the inside of the Bitch Helmet nervously, her germaphobia kicking in as she wondered how many other women had ridden bitch on his motorcycle and worn this helmet. She sighed and pulled it over her hair, struggling to clasp the chin straps together.

"Let me help you." His hands were now on her neck, buckling the strap in place, while his lips were just inches from hers again. "Alright, hop on."

She straddled him on the back of the bike, her inner thighs pressed up against his outer thighs. For the first time, she could get a good look at the back of his vest, and the detail of the insignia on it. In bright red letters, it said, "ARMY OF OUTLAWS MC," and then underneath the cowboy skull and crossbones in smaller letters, "CENTRAL COAST CHAPTER."

So, she was right about them.

"What does the writing on your vest mean?" She tried the playing dumb approach.

"My what?"

She opened her mouth to speak but wasn't sure how to rephrase her question.

"Vest?" He craned his neck to glare back at her over his right shoulder. "I'm not a fucking valet, or one of those guys at the airport who waves planes down. I don't wear vests. This is a cut."

"Oh," she said. "What's the difference?"

He laughed. "Time to go, sweetheart."

She braced herself and leaned in to wrap her arms around him, smelling his strangely erotic combination of fresh laundry and body odor, feeling the divots of his abs under his t-shirt as she awkwardly navigated where to hold him. He laughed, taking her hands in his and moving them up to his chest, showing her how to correctly interlock her fingers.

The engine revving startled her, and Hayden yelled, "Hold on tight," as they sped off down the street. She immediately felt like she was going to fall off and exercised every ounce of self-control not to ask him to slow down.

She'd been imagining this moment since the day she moved in next door, but in her fantasy, it had been so much calmer, easier, breezier. A background of sepia-toned beachscapes, a romantic scene out of a Lana Del Rey music video, her body draped around his.

In real life, it was terrifying, blustery, and painful to keep her fingers interlocked at full speed. The only thing separating her from injury or death was the strength in her hands and arms. *Thank god for all that yoga.*

They rode for another 30 minutes before Hayden finally pulled down a windy, unmarked road that led out to a cliff overlooking the ocean. Was he trying to make a move on her, in front of this picturesque ocean lookout?

When they passed a "No Fishing" sign, Hayden veered left off the main road and down what looked like a recently man-made trail in a clearing of brush. And as they rode further off-road into the rural cliff area, she was starting to wonder if maybe she'd judged the situation wrong.

Was he bringing her there to...hurt her? After all, what did she really know about him? He was in a motorcycle club, a club that had been rumored to be organized crime—basically a mafia—with ties (according to Wikipedia) to sex trafficking, drug dealing, arms dealing, gambling, and some mysterious disappearances of people tied to their circles (although no formal murder charges had ever been filed, that she could find). Hayden lived with other club members, who referred to him as El Jefe, meaning he was in charge to some degree. He'd kidnapped, beaten, and imprisoned a man in his shed for the past several weeks. And she was a witness to all of that. A liability. Maybe this whole flirtation was just a trap to get her out into the wilderness to get rid of her, get rid of the evidence.

They slowed down enough to where she could make conversation if she yelled over the rumbling motor.

"So, are you ever going to tell me what the deal is with the guy you're keeping in your backyard?" she yelled into his ear.

He was silent for a moment, and she worried she'd overstepped. *I'm a liability.*

"I thought we trusted each other, neighbor," he yelled back.

"We do," she said.

"Can't you just trust then that he deserves to be where he is?"

"I guess..."

"Don't worry. I'm not dragging you out here to murder you."

Was he a mind reader?

"Good, because Craig put a tracking device in my shoulder just in case of emergencies," she joked.

"Oh, those are easy to just cut out of your skin."

Silence.

As they rode further into the clearing, the main road disappeared behind them, and she now saw dozens of motorcycles and several cars and trucks parked near a giant tree. Behind the tree, a group of around 30 people was gathered, drinking and being rowdy.

"Where are we?" she yelled into Hayden's ear, realizing they'd slowed down enough that she didn't need to yell anymore.

"A party."

He shifted into neutral as they neared the tree. She was starting to regret this decision. She'd signed up for exploring this dangerous world of Hayden. She hadn't signed up for meeting all his friends. She was feeling very self-conscious all the sudden.

They parked at the end of the row of bikes, and she quickly unsnapped her helmet and ripped it off her head, pleading with the gods that she didn't have horrible helmet hair. She quickly shook her hair out and fluffed her roots with her fingertips before Hayden had a chance to turn around and look at her.

He helped her off the bike and did a onceover on her body.

"Still in one piece, that's good. How was your first ride?"

"My arms hurt." She laughed.

"They'll get used to it the more you ride."

Does that mean he wants this to happen again? She suddenly wished she'd brought a secret stash of booze. *A little liquid courage would be great right about now.*

They walked toward the crowd of people in the clearing. Many of the men were wearing the Army of Outlaws *cuts* and the women seemed to be wearing all black. It was a sea of strange, dark ensembles—black dresses, black skirts, black netted rave shirts, black leather skirts with fishnet tights, black jumpsuits.

Thank god I decided to wear a black shirt. Impulsively, she flipped her diamond ring under her finger, a half-assed attempt to make her marital status less obvious.

Country music was playing from a speaker somewhere, and there was a large picnic table set up with dozens of dishes in varying containers, like a potluck. She spotted a large bucket of ice filled with beers and eyed it longingly. As they came upon the large gathering, several people noticed Hayden and walked over to greet him.

"Hayden! So glad you're here, bro," a large—vertically and horizontally—man with a long, chest-length beard said as he walked up to give Hayden a bear hug. "My mom will be really happy to see you. She's over there."

Blake looked to where the large man had nodded and saw a woman in her mid-50s sitting in a camping chair with a black veil over her face. Two men in Army of Outlaws paraphernalia and a younger red-headed girl stood behind her, hands on her shoulders, comforting her. The woman in the veil was shaking with sobs. The scene looked like a fucked-up biker version of *American Gothic.*

"Kelly was family to me," Hayden said to his large friend. "You know we're doing everything to get justice."

The large man's eyes filled with tears as he choked them back into a pseudo cough. "Thanks, man. Glad you're here."

After the large man walked away, Blake turned to Hayden. "Umm, is this...a funeral?"

"A wake, actually."

"What the hell?" she said louder than she'd intended. She lowered her volume. "Why would you bring me to a wake? This is so awkward and...inappropriate."

"Don't worry, it's more of a memorial. There's no body or anything." He playfully shoved her. "Just an excuse for everyone to get together and drink around a bonfire."

"Still. Are you sure it's not weird that I'm here?"

"You wanted to ride, didn't you? You have to be up for anything when you ride with me."

As she worked on a clever retort, his eyes wandered to the grieving woman in the veil. He turned back to face her. "I'm gonna go make the rounds. Why don't you go find yourself a beverage and make some friends?"

Before she could respond, he walked away from her. She was furious. Why did she agree to this stupid adventure? Now she was stuck in the middle of nowhere with a huge crowd of grieving gangsters, with no escape in sight. It would have been one thing if she was a young, single 20-something, up for adventure for the sake of impressing a guy she liked. But she was a married woman in her 30s. She got married so she didn't have to do things like this anymore. And looking around at this rough crowd reminded her just how out of place she was. Maybe she was almost dressed for the part, but there was no way she'd have anything in common with these people. And so far, none of them had bothered to introduce themselves.

She pulled her phone out of her purse, desperate for something to keep her occupied, and saw she had notifications from Craig and Jasmine.

Craig: Hey babe, made it to my hotel in Downtown LA and am heading out to meet the investors for dinner. I'll text you later to tell you all the dumb things they say. {Winking tongue-out emoji}

Jasmine: Hey girl! What happened to you the other day? You hung up so abruptly, I thought maybe I upset you by talking about work too much. Anyway, thinking of you. Call me when you want to catch up more xoxo

"You look like you need a drink," a familiar voice said. She looked up from her phone to see Red standing in front of her, grinning wide at the sight of her being at one of their gatherings.

"Oh, thank god," she said. "Yes, please."

She followed Red to the big bucket of booze and chose the beer that looked like it had the highest alcohol content.

"Nice choice," Red acknowledged, cheersing her beer with his.

"So, whose wake is this?" she asked him.

Red laughed. "You mean Hayden brought you all the way here and didn't even tell you why? Sounds like him."

She sipped her beer, waiting for him to elaborate.

"Kelly... She was one of our own. Part of our tribe. She was only 18 years old. And this motherfucking pervert raped and murdered her last month."

"Oh my god..." she replied, not knowing how to process or respond to that.

"Yeah. We were all like big brothers to her. Supposed to protect her from shit like that." He took a long swig of his beer.

"What private information are you sharing with this random chick?" Dave jumped in, apparently overhearing what Red was saying and feeling the need to intervene.

"She's not random. She's—"

"—Our neighbor, I know." Dave looked at her, scrutinizing her. "Just...be careful, man. Don't get yourself in trouble just because you like the way a girl looks."

"Hey, I'm standing right here," she said, offended by the way they talked about her in third person.

"We can see that, sweetheart," Dave said. "You're hard to miss."

Red redirected the conversation and turned to Dave, saying, "Our neighbor was just telling me she thinks she can drink me under the table." She eyed Red suspiciously.

"Is that right?" Dave asked, amused now. "Alright, let's see which one of you can finish their beer faster."

"But isn't this...like...a funeral?" she asked stupidly.

"Honey, you know jack shit about us," Elvis chimed in with an affected drawl, walking toward them to join their little circle. "This isn't a regular wake."

The rest of the group chuckled and cheersed each other.

"So, we doing this or what, neighbor?" Red asked her.

She carefully looked around and saw more club members were eyeing their group. A few women had taken notice of her and were watching her closely. One cluster of particularly intimidating-looking biker chicks smirked as one of them whispered something to the others.

"Hell yeah," Blake said confidently. She did another scan of the area, searching for Hayden. He was nowhere to be found.

"Ohhh, it's on then!" Dave was visibly buzzed. "Alright. Red, neighbor—"

"—Blake," she corrected.

"Mmhmm. Red, Blake. On the count of three," Dave commanded.

"Wait!" Elvis jumped in. "They can't play with half-empty beers. Let's get them some fresh ones."

Once they were beered up, the contest began.

"3, 2, 1, CHUG!"

Blake was wiping the residual beer from her mouth after emptying an entire bottle by the time Red had even made it three fourths of the way through his own beer.

"Damn, Blake! You can hold your own," Dave commented as he and Elvis gave her an accepting nod. "Red, you're a real disappointment of a man. You should probably just go home."

The games continued until dusk.

"Let's play some crip cup while the prospects get the bonfire going," Red suggested to their now larger group, which now included two of the provocatively-dressed women whom Blake recognized from their parties.

"Blake, you're on my team!" Dave declared, throwing a heavy arm around her shoulder.

"What's crip cup?" Blake asked.

"It's what you think it is." Dave smiled.

"Hold up," one of the women, a tiny wafer of a human, said to the group. Her black skirt was so low risen that her exposed belly button ring sparkled bright above it. She must have weighed 100 pounds, at most. "I've gotta pee. Any of you need the ladies' room?" She looked around at the other women.

"Actually, I do," Blake said, suddenly aware of how full her bladder was from the beer chugging.

"Alright, new girl. Let's go," she said.

"I'll come too," the other woman, a much taller bleach-blonde wearing a corset that pushed her boobs up to her chin, said to them.

"Why do women always go to the bathroom together?" Red pondered.

"Hurry back, sweet cheeks!" Dave called to the three women as they walked away.

She was anxious to see what kind of a "ladies' room" situation they'd be working with in this remote, wilderness pop-up party. She was also nervous about being alone with these two women who hadn't said a word directly to her or introduced themselves the entire time they'd been playing games.

As they walked farther away from the guys who lived next door to her, she noticed a group of older, scarier-looking men, all with a look in their eyes like they'd lived a thousand more lives than she had. Through their sunglasses and rugged beards, donning their Army of Outlaws cuts, they eyed her suspiciously as she walked by them, singling her out from the other women. She could feel their stares penetrating her back as she kept walking. Who were these older men?

"I'm Blake, by the way." She turned back to the women beside her, deciding to take the lead.

The women looked her up and down as they walked alongside her.

"Brittany," the tiny wafer said.

"Nikki," the taller blonde said.

"Isn't Blake a boy's name?" Nikki asked, sniffling like she had a cold.

"Sometimes," Blake said.

"No, you dumbass," Brittany said to Nikki. "What about Blake Lively?"

"Oh yeah," Nikki laughed. "Ohmygod, I used to love *Gossip Girl*. Those rich bitches were crazy."

"So, are there actual bathrooms here? Or are we squatting somewhere?" Blake asked.

"There's a thing of port-a-potties just down this way," Brittany said, pointing in front of them.

Blake tried not to cringe.

"This seems like a good spot to re-up though," Nikki said to Brittany, pulling a little plastic bag from between her corset cleavage.

"Oh, hit me!" Brittany said excitedly.

Nikki unsealed the bag and dug a little miniature spoon on a chain out of it, wrapping the chain securely around her wrist. Blake could see in the now moonlight that the spoon was covered in white powder residue. Hovering in close, Brittany watched hungrily as Nikki dipped the spoon in the bag and then brought it up to one of her nostrils, snorting it loudly. Then, it was Brittany's turn. Nikki dipped the spoon back into the bag and carefully held it out toward Brittany's face as Brittany placed an index finger over one of her nostrils and sniffed hard through the other.

"Want a bump?" Nikki turned to Blake, holding up the spoon.

Blake had done cocaine in her younger partying days, but she had no idea what this substance was or where it came from. She was way too nervous to chance it, so she declined politely. "I'm good, thanks. But you guys go ahead!"

"So, what's the deal with you and Hayden?" Brittany asked Blake, placing her nose back over the spoon in Nikki's hand to do another bump. She sniffed. "Are you guys fucking?"

Blake was caught off guard by the directness of the question. "Umm, no, absolutely not. We're just neighbors. I'm actually married."

Brittany and Nikki's eyes both shot straight to Blake's left hand.

"What, he couldn't afford a diamond?" Nikki said, pointing to the simple gold band.

"Oh," Blake said, embarrassed. "Guess it flipped around somehow." She turned the diamond back to the top and both Brittany and Nikki gasped.

"Damn, girl! Nevermind. Keep him, whoever he is."

"Thanks, I think I will," Blake said.

Nikki did another bump from the spoon. "I fucked Hayden once," she said casually.

"When?" Brittany asked angrily. "Was it before or after the night that I gave him a blowjob?"

"Definitely before." Nikki laughed. "You know I never do sloppy seconds."

"You cunt!" Brittany playfully shoved her friend. Both of their eyes were wide and fiery from the drugs.

Cool. Is there anyone at this party that Hayden hasn't had sex with?

"Yeah, well it doesn't matter anyway. Lately he's been all over that Christina ho from Oxnard. That girl is a train wreck."

Blake wondered if Christina was the woman she'd seen Hayden with in his room that night.

"I think she's pretty." Nikki shrugged.

"Aww, thanks, girl," a new woman's voice said sarcastically from behind them.

Blake turned around and saw a beautiful woman with long, dark hair walking toward them. The woman from Hayden's bedroom. Christina.

"Nice to know I have a fan among a sea of bitches," Christina said, adjusting her super short dress that clung to her perfectly curved body.

"Who you calling a bitch?" Brittany the 100-pound-wafer challenged her, rage surging in her face. She puffed her anorexic chest out at Christina, clearly ready to fight.

"Calm down," Christina said, unfazed. "I just came over here to pee. Not looking for trouble."

"Damn right," Brittany said, waving her off. Christina eyed Blake suspiciously as she walked away from them.

"Yeah, I'm gonna pee too," Blake said, feeling her bladder about to explode. After braving the outhouse, she walked back out to see Brittany and Nikki huddled together again.

"Ok, just *one* more hit, and then let's go back," Nikki was saying to Brittany. After the two girls had gotten sufficiently high, the three of them walked back toward the gathering of people. Christina had seemingly disappeared.

When they returned to the larger group, the bonfire had grown significantly since they'd left, and everyone seemed drunker.

"LADIES!" Red yelled to them. "Where you been? It's time to play."

They rejoined the circle to line up for the game. Dave threw an arm around Blake's shoulder again without permission, more forward and direct with her. She was on guard with him. He had this bristly mustache that seemed to perpetually have beer foam stuck in it, and he was crude. But she was grateful for the attention and hoped that Hayden would see. Maybe even get jealous.

"Alright, drink!" Dave yelled, as the teams launched into playing the game. *Ah, so crip cup is just...flip cup.*

Maybe some of these guys weren't so different from the types of people she knew. Maybe they weren't as intimidating as she'd originally thought. They were basically...frat boys. Minus the school. Well, at least the younger guys were. The older club members still frightened her. They had a harder, harsher appearance to them. Danger vibes. Behind her, Blake overheard a conversation that pulled her in like a magnet.

"It's that motherfucker, Hector," one man was saying. "He set up a new casino after the last one got shut down. The Desperados are entering dangerous territory, setting up their shady business on our turf."

Hector. She reeled at the name. *So, Craig's moved on from his old days at the horse races to something much sketchier.*

She casually stole a glance behind her to see who was having the conversation. It was Rocco, the scary guy from her neigh-

77

bors' house with the burly beard, pitted acne scars, and bald head. She didn't recognize the second man, but he looked older. Maybe in his 50s.

"So, what are we gonna do about it?" the older man said. "We can't let him get away with it."

"Blake, look alive!" Dave pointed to her cup to motion that it was her turn to flip it. She chugged the flat beer down and flipped it on the first try (thanks, college education), which caused Dave to cheer loudly and pick her up by her legs to pull her up above his head.

"Alright, that's enough!" she screamed down at him through laughter. He finally placed her back on the ground and gave her ass a light slap. "Go team!"

She rolled her eyes but didn't tell him he'd crossed a line. She wasn't prepared to piss off a group of drunk bikers.

As she turned away from drunken Dave, she was startled by a hard fist pounding down on the crip cup table. The older guy who'd been talking to Rocco was standing there, fuming.

"That's enough of this disrespectful child's play. This is a wake, for *gods sakes*. Show some respect."

Everyone was silent, clearly spooked. The man turned to Dave and violently knocked the red cup out of his hand, sending the beer dregs flying into the grass.

"I'm sorry, man," Dave said sheepishly, nervous. "We didn't mean any disrespect."

"Stop with this fucking frat party shit. Just because you're third generation doesn't mean you can embarrass yourself—or the club." The older man's tone was threatening, commanding. Once effectively killing the vibe, he shook his head in disgust, glaring at each of them before storming away into the darkness. The rest of the group stood around awkwardly, trying to resuscitate the party without the game.

"You look like you need saving." Hayden's voice was in her ear, his breath hot on her cold neck.

"What makes you say that?" she said, without turning around. She caught a glimpse of Rocco and his unidentified friend staring at her from the other side of the firepit. Rocco looked predatory, like he might jump out and attack her at any moment.

Hayden spun her around to face him and wiped spilled beer from her chin with his thumb. "If you're not careful, these guys *will* make you black out."

"Hey," Red shot back. "We can hear you, you know."

"I know you can. Stop overserving the women, or they're gonna stop coming to our parties." Hayden pressed his finger-tips into her lower back and guided her away from the group.

"Blake, you're a goddess!" Dave yelled at her as they walked away, apparently her friend now. "Come party with us anytime."

Hayden led them to a quiet place farther away from the group, but where they could still feel the warmth of the fire. He handed her the jacket she'd stashed in his bike, a surprisingly thoughtful gesture. He then took off his own jacket and laid it on the ground, motioning for her to sit.

"Really, Hayden?" she asked, sliding her arms into her jacket. Now that they were away from everyone else, she allowed herself to become incredulous. "You dragged me to the wilderness, to a funeral, without telling me the plan, and then left me on my own for hours. Why should I sit down with you?"

"Because... I'm sorry?" He batted his beautiful dark lashes which caressed his piercing blue eyes. She hated that it worked.

"Come on," he said, patting the ground next to him again. "I promise I'm yours the rest of the night."

She sighed and sat down next to him, cross-legged on his jacket.

"I see you made some friends." He was smiling mischievously at her.

"I'm a big girl," she said. "I don't need to be babysat."

"Clearly," he said. "Thanks for being cool. Had to go pay my respects to the grieving mother."

"I'm sorry for your loss," she said, disarmed by his comment. "I can't even imagine."

"Karma is a bitch. He's getting his."

"Getting?"

"I feel pretty confident." He reached into his pocket and pulled out a flask, taking a swig from it. "Want something a little stronger than that Mexican piss beer?"

She nodded and took the flask from him, their hands grazing momentarily. She threw her head back as she swigged the mystery liquid, quickly realizing it was whiskey and that she hated whiskey. She held back a choking cough and tried to look cool, handing the flask back to him.

"You're really beautiful. Do you know that?"

His compliment caught her by surprise, and the burning whiskey in the back of her throat finally made its way to her lungs, sending her into a coughing fit. She turned her head away from him as she let it out.

"I mean...maybe not now," he teased, as she coughed out her lungs.

"Shut." *Cough.* "Up." *Cough.* She laughed as her fit subsided, and playfully pushed his chest away.

He placed his hand gently on her knee, careful of the bandages beneath the denim, lightly rubbing his hand up her thigh. Instant chills. In the romantic dim lighting of the fire, he leaned in, putting his mouth torturously close to hers. His lips parted slightly. This was it.

"Craig's cheating on me," she blurted, breaking the trance.

Hayden pulled his face back, surprise in his eyes. He didn't say anything.

"Yeah, I found a burner phone in one of his running shoes the other day. And then I followed him to her house and saw them together." Word vomit. She couldn't stop it. She took the flask back and took another swig of the dreaded whiskey. Swallowing and roughly clearing her throat, she continued, "Some woman named Kendra."

"Sounds like a stripper name," Hayden joked. When he saw Blake wasn't laughing, he reached an arm out and draped it over her shoulder, pulling her into him. They stayed there for a moment, cuddled up.

"I'm sorry," he finally said. "That guy is a fucking idiot if he's cheating on you. You're a TEN."

She pulled out of his embrace and squinted at him. "You know, I've always hated that ranking system. It's so misogynistic and problematic."

"That's a lot of big words." He grinned wide, accentuating his perfect dimples. "So, do you want me to take care of him for you?"

"You mean...'take care of him' in like a sleeping with the fishes kind of way?"

"I mean I wouldn't put it in such a dorky way," he laughed, "but yeah. Maybe that's what I mean. What do you think?"

"Maybe I'd like that," she said, the alcohol really kicking in. She allowed herself to snuggle back into his shoulder again as they stared out at the bonfire, with all the bikers and grieving women in black partying around it.

"Hayden," she said, finally ready to explore this strange attraction.

"Yes, TEN?"

"Sorry to interrupt," a female voice said behind them. Blake and Hayden turned to see Christina standing over them, rubbing her bare arms. "Hayden, mind if I grab my truck keys? I'm freezing and need my jacket."

"Of course, sweetheart." Hayden reached into his jeans pocket and pulled out a set of keys, tossing them up to her. She caught them with ease.

"Thanks for holding onto them. I don't have any pockets," she said, suggestively running her hands down the sides of her skintight dress. She lingered a moment to give Blake another onceover, full smirk on display, and then bounced off toward the area where all the vehicles were parked. So, Hayden had hung out with her at some point during the party, long enough for her to have him hold her keys. What was his deal? Why did he even bring her here, to this sea of women practically begging to hook up with him?

"You have a lot of fans around here," Blake said, affecting her best flirty laugh.

"What's that mean?" Hayden asked.

"Girls talk," she teased.

"And are you a fan?"

"I don't know yet," she said, tilting her head. "Depends on if you kill me on the ride home tonight."

"That's fair," he said.

The moment had passed, and it didn't seem like he was going to make a move.

"You ready to go home?" he asked her, placing his hand on her shoulders, and rubbing to keep her warm. His touch was like a drug to her. It felt so wrong, but she couldn't get enough.

"Thought you'd never ask."

The ride home was freezing, and she was grateful he'd insisted she bring a jacket. As they finally cruised into his side yard before parking and turning the engine off, she was relieved the ride was over. Then it hit her. It was her first time being in Hayden's yard.

"Well, you survived an entire day with me," he said as he slid off the bike. He held out a hand for her, and she took it to help her dismount. "Congratulations."

"'Survived' is the bar you set for women you spend time with?"

"I mean I'd hope for 'enjoyed' too, but I didn't want to assume."

She thought about this for a moment. "I enjoyed...parts of it."

"Which parts were those?" he asked as he moved in to unbuckle her helmet. His fingers grazed her chin, and she'd never wanted to be kissed so badly.

"The parts where you were actually there."

"Mrs. Davis," he teased. "Do you have a crush on me?"

"Don't call me that," she said, suddenly ashamed. "It's too weird. This whole thing is weird."

"I'm sorry." He pulled the helmet off her head and placed it on one of the handles. "For the record, I have a crush on you too."

"What are we, 16?" She laughed.

"Would you rather me tell you that I find you unbearably sexy, and that I've been obsessing over what your naked body

83

looked like from afar, and wanting to see what it looks like up close, for weeks?"

She bit her lip. Was this finally it? "Well, then, why don't you make that happen?"

He smiled mysteriously, stepping back from her. "Nah, I don't think so."

"What?" She was suddenly feeling rejected.

"I'd like to see you naked, but I also don't think it's a good idea to fuck my neighbor's wife. Even if he is having an affair." Then he smiled again. "Maybe especially because he's having an affair. Too much drama."

She couldn't argue with that. But she wanted this to happen. Finally, she gave into her animal instinct and rushed toward him, pressing her body into his and tilting her face up to meet his eyes. "Then can you at least kiss me? Clothes on?"

His smile widened and he leaned his face in, gently kissing her on the lips. He tasted like whiskey and cinnamon. They kissed for several more seconds before he pulled away and playfully pushed her off him.

"Alright, got your fix then?" He winked at her, his blue eyes searing.

"Definitely not." She laughed back. "But I agree with you that this is a bad idea."

"A hot, bad idea," he teased.

He was so confusing. Did he want to sleep with her or not?

"Come here," he finally said, holding his arms out. She did as she was told. He pulled her into a tight hug, their bodies fully embraced from head to toe. His belt buckle pressed into her stomach, and she could smell the sweat on his leather cut, which was somehow like pheromones to her. They stood like that for a while before she finally released herself from the embrace and backed up a few steps.

"Alright, well I'm gonna go inside then." She walked toward the gate. "Thanks for a really...strange day."

"Hey, wait."

She turned back to face him.

"Wanna come over for a nightcap?"

"Absolutely."

She followed him into his backyard and up the steps to the back door. As he unlocked and opened the door, she glanced over her shoulder at the shed, and wondered if the man was still alive in there. From this angle, she realized the shed was clearly much larger than she'd originally thought, about the size of a small garage. Fighting the part of her that wanted to run and hide, she followed Hayden inside.

The house was quiet, seemingly empty. Everyone was probably still at the wake. She looked around—there was a confederate flag hanging on one of the walls. *Yikes.* Jasmine would be horrified. As a woman of color and activist for dismantling systemic racism, she'd tell Blake to get the hell out of that house and never look back at these white supremacist gang bangers. The house also looked and smelled like a disaster. Like a frat house. There were empty beer bottles on most of the surfaces around the living room and weird stains on the carpet. *Maybe this is a bad idea.*

"Don't worry. My room doesn't look like this." He smiled, reading her mind. He took her hand. "Come on."

She knew there was no turning back now, despite her danger radar blaring. They walked into the living room and up the 1970s carpeted stairs, landing at a hallway. There were what looked like endless doors, all closed with padlocks and plaques with names on them. She followed Hayden, hand in his hand, past four doors until they came to his: Hayden Christ.

"I'm sorry. Your last name is *Christ*?" she asked abruptly.

"It's pronounced KR-I-ST actually. Like 'crisp' with a 't' at the end."

"Oh good. Wouldn't want you to have a Jesus complex or anything," she teased.

"Not unless you count these hard-earned abs, baby," he said as he lifted his white shirt to show off his body.

"Ew gross," she mocked, rolling her eyes, even though the sight of his bare abs thrilled her.

He smiled knowingly as he let go of his shirt and reached into his jeans pocket for a key. As he unlocked the door to his bedroom, Blake panicked. It was all becoming so real. This was happening. Now she wasn't sure if she could do it, after everything.

He opened the door and waved his arm for her to enter. "Ladies first."

She walked into the room, suddenly aware of her body, holding her arms across her chest insecurely.

"I always love when a woman looks uncomfortable in my space," he joked.

"Sorry, I just sort of realized where I am...and what this means." She let herself take in the scene surrounding her. His room, like he'd said, didn't resemble the frat house mess downstairs. It was immaculate, well-furnished, and decorated even. It looked like a grown-up's room. With a grown-up bed. It smelled clean and inviting. And there were no symbols of racism on display, not that she could find at first glance anyway.

"What does it mean?" he asked, walking over to a bar set up in the corner of the room to pour drinks for them. Blake wandered over to a wall with framed photos hanging on it and looked at the smiling faces of Hayden and his friends, all in their matching cuts, standing next to their motorcycles.

"I'm a married woman in the bedroom of a man who isn't my husband," she said.

"So, go then," he said, holding out a glass with brown liquid (probably more whiskey) for her to take.

She took the glass and sat down on his bed.

"Or not." He smiled. Turning away from her, he grabbed a chair from his desk, and spun it around, straddling it to face her. He sipped his drink.

"No cheers?" she asked, holding her drink out. He didn't reciprocate.

"What do you want, Blake?" he asked instead.

She pulled her drink back, realizing there would be no cheers. She took a sip. *Yep, definitely whiskey.* She swallowed, trying not to make a face. "What do I want?"

"Yes."

"I don't know what you mean."

"I mean that your husband is cheating on you. You're over at my house, in my bedroom. You kissed me." He smiled at that. "Are you looking for a revenge fuck?"

She stared at him for a second. "Why do you always have to be so direct?"

"How I roll."

"I don't know what I'm looking for." She sighed. "But you trying to get me to say it out loud makes me feel ashamed."

"Well, I don't want you to feel ashamed because of me," he said. "But I also don't want drama knocking on my door."

He set his drink down on his desk and stood from his chair, walking toward her and sitting next to her on the bed. He looked into her eyes and touched a strand of her blonde hair that had fallen into her face, lightly grabbing it and tucking it behind her ear. Just like Craig had always done. Her discomfort escalated into anxiety.

"I can't get naked with you," she blurted out.

He immediately pulled his hand away from her face.

"Alright." He placed both hands around his glass, setting them in his lap. "Then I guess I'll repeat my question, Blake. What do you want?"

She bit her lip and looked down at her own glass. "Can we..." She looked up into his eyes, as piercing as always. "Can we, like, talk for a bit?"

Hayden laughed. "Sure," he said, getting up from the bed and walking over to the bar to pour himself more whiskey. "I have to say this is a first, having a girl in my bedroom and *not* fucking her."

"And I'm suddenly grossed out to be sitting on your comforter," she said, laughing.

Hayden walked toward her with the bottle and refilled her already full glass. "You should be," he said.

"Yikes." She stood up from the bed, but Hayden lightly pushed her back down.

"Oh, calm down, lady. I'm kidding."

Her heartbeat had sped up from the play fight, but she didn't want to give into her urges. "So where did you grow up?" She cringed at herself for the small talk.

"SoCal born and raised. You?"

"Denver," she answered. "But I moved to Arizona for college and pretty much stayed there until moving here last month."

"Is this really what you had in mind by 'talking?'" he asked. He sat back down in his chair to face her.

"I panicked." She smiled.

"So then talk to me about something real."

"Ok." Her brain was spinning and suddenly all she could think about was Hector. She wanted to ask Hayden about him but didn't want him to know she'd heard the name from him or his friends. She needed to tread lightly. "I found something else in Craig's phone," she finally said. "*Someone* else. Besides Kendra."

"Two chicks?" He seemed impressed.

"No. A guy actually."

Hayden raised an eyebrow in amusement.

"Not like that," she said, taking a sip of her whiskey. It was starting to grow on her. "He owes this guy money. I read through the texts, and this guy...Hector...said if he didn't pay up that there would be consequences."

She looked up into Hayden's eyes to search for recognition, but Hayden held his steady gaze without so much as flinching.

"Anyway, the day that he was supposed to pay, he came home with his face swollen and covered in bruises. Said he was mugged."

"Doesn't sound like that to me," Hayden said.

"What do you mean?"

"Sounds like he suffered those 'consequences,'" Hayden said matter-of-factly.

She stared at him. "Do you really think that?"

"I mean," he said, pausing. "I don't know what things are like in Arizona, but around here people who make a living collecting on debts don't fuck around."

"What makes you think this was someone from Arizona?" she asked.

He looked confused. "Well, you just moved here. How could he already owe money to someone out here?"

"This woman, this...Kendra. She lives here, and Craig started seeing her two months before we moved here. He was regularly coming out here to start transitioning into his new job."

"So, you think Hector is someone local?" Hayden looked more concerned now.

"I think so."

"Do you have any more information on this guy? Any mention of specific local places?"

"No. Just that Craig owed him money," she said, trying to remember any helpful details. "I mean he did say 'you're playing with fire' in one of his texts to Craig, but that's a pretty common saying."

Hayden's blue eyes widened.

"You're sure his name is Hector?" he asked, his face serious.

"That's what he was saved as in Craig's contacts," she said. "Why? Do you know who it is?"

"I think so," he said, looking away from her, sipping his whiskey.

When he didn't say anything else, she finally asked, "Want to elaborate?"

"If it's who I think it is, then your husband is a way bigger piece of shit than I thought. And he might have put you in danger."

"Umm, what?" she asked, standing up from the bed. "What do you mean by danger?"

Hayden was silent, eyeing her carefully.

When he didn't respond, she knew she wasn't going to get any more out of him unless she was bolder. She decided to take a chance on Hayden.

"I heard some guys at the wake talking about someone named Hector. They said something about a casino? And what was it?

The...*Desperados*? Is that the same person?"

"Yeah," Hayden said. "I think it might be."

"What does that mean? What kind of danger am I in?"

"Don't worry, little lady," Hayden said, his voice returning to its normal calm and collected state. He walked toward her, closing the gap between them, and pulled her body into his, wrapping his arms around her. "The good news is you live next door to me, and I won't let anything bad happen to you." He kissed the top of her head, and she felt woozy—from the embrace, from the staggering news about her husband's double life, from the fear of being attacked by this stranger named Hector.

"Who are the Desperados?" she asked, her head buried in his shoulder.

"They're my enemies," Hayden said stoically.

She pulled out of his embrace. "I'm sorry," she said, a smile creeping onto her face. "I'm gonna need you to give me a little more than that. Your *enemies*?"

He smiled back. "They're a Mexican motorcycle club. Their main hustle is gambling, and they run a lot of underground casinos."

"That doesn't sound that scary," she said.

"Oh sweetheart, you have no idea," he said. "They are very dangerous. And well connected with the cartel."

"Shit."

"Yeah."

They stared at each other for a minute, neither of them speaking.

"It's probably best if you stay here tonight," Hayden finally said. "I don't want you all alone in that house."

"I don't know about that," she said, looking down at the

ground.

"You were ready to jump my bones five minutes ago, and now I offer for you to stay here and be protected, and you're ready to leave? *Women*."

They both laughed.

"Tell you what," he said. "You take my bed, and I'll sleep on one of the couches downstairs."

"No, that's ridiculous," she said. "We can...both sleep in here."

"Oh yeah, missy?"

"Yeah."

"Alright, well if you wake up to something hard poking you in the back, it's just my ultimate sexual frustration saying hello."

After Hayden gave her a t-shirt to sleep in, they climbed into his bed and got under the covers. They smelled just like him, and she wanted to roll around in them and get his scent all over her.

They assumed an appropriate, spaced-out spooning position, her the little and him the big, until he suddenly pulled her body in close to his, holding her in his arms.

"Is this ok?" he asked.

She literally wanted to die, it was so ok.

"It's ok," she finally said.

"Good." He kissed the top of her head again. "Goodnight, neighbor."

Chapter 8

She woke up to the sound of heavy breathing. Slowly opening her eyes, she squinted into the bright light flooding the room.

"Craig?" she mumbled sleepily before her eyes adjusted more and she suddenly remembered where she was. *Ohmygod.*

She shot up in the bed, arms flying to her chest, where one boob had popped out of the loose-fitting t-shirt Hayden had given her. She readjusted the shirt to cover herself, peering over the edge of the bed where the heavy breathing was coming from. Hayden was on the floor next to the bed, doing push-ups shirtless with earbuds in his ears.

"Hayden!" she called. He didn't hear her and continued his aggressive workout. She leaned over and tapped him on the shoulder. He jumped at her touch, falling onto his forearms.

"Jesus." He looked up at her, taking the earbuds out of his ears. "Don't sneak up on a guy with earbuds in."

"Sorry," she said, not able to resist looking at his ridiculous abs again.

He noticed her looking and smiled, feigning modesty by crossing his arms in front of him. "How dare you objectify me like that, neighbor?"

"I literally just woke up." She laughed. "Not my fault you're half naked and glistening in front of me."

"Well, then you're welcome." He curled his tongue up to the left corner of his lips and smiled playfully at her. "I'm glad you're awake. I gotta run to a thing in a minute."

"Oh, right," she said, scanning the room looking for her clothes. "I'll get out of your hair then." She waited for him to say something nice in response, but when he was silent, she quickly jumped out of bed and walked over to where she'd spotted her clothes from the day before.

"Do you mind?" she asked, motioning for him to turn around so she could safely put her clothes back on.

"Nothing I haven't seen before," he smirked, "but you got it." He turned away from her and went back to doing his push-ups, sans headphones. *Show off.*

"Hey, by the way," she said uneasily.

"Yeah?" he asked without pausing on the push-ups.

"You know I was just kidding last night about the 'taking care of my husband' thing, right?"

He stopped mid push-up and dropped to his knees. Looking up at her, he smiled deviously. "Of course. Respect thy neighbor, and all that."

"You would say that, Mr. Christ," she teased. He smiled but didn't respond, returning instead to his push-ups. *Seriously, how many of those is he going to do?* Once she was dressed, she walked over to his desk to grab her purse. "Alright, I'm going to head home."

"Alright, sweetheart." He used the momentum from his push-up to propel him effortlessly into a standing position. "I'd give you a hug but...I'm all '*glistening.*'"

"That's ok." She laughed. "Thank you for your protection last night."

"I always use protection."

She rolled her eyes. "Alright, how do I get out of here?"

"C'mon, I'll walk you out," he said, leading her out of the bedroom, still shirtless and sweaty. Downstairs there were a few other guys sitting in the living room watching TV. Dave looked up when he heard them coming, and when he saw that it was Hayden with Blake, he looked visibly disappointed.

"Well, look who's doing the walk of shame," he said loudly, causing the other bikers to look up and stare at them too.

"It's not a wal—" Blake started, but Hayden interrupted her.

"Mind your own business, you circle jerks."

"Not without El Jefe here to lead the circle jerk," Red joked back.

"Alright, alright, show's over. Get back to your Netflix," Hayden said, leading Blake to the front door. She glanced over at the coffee table in front of the men. There were two black handguns splayed out, casually sitting next to a coffee mug and four empty beer bottles. Her heart skipped a beat.

"Actually," she said, quieting her voice to a whisper. "Mind if I go out the back door?"

"Ohhhhh," Red cheered, overhearing her whisper. "It *is* a walk of shame. She doesn't even want to be seen with you, bro."

"Watch your mouth, *bro*," Hayden said. Red's smile faded and he turned back to the TV, quiet.

"Come on, neighbor," Hayden said to Blake, steering her toward the back door.

"Hey, do me a favor?" Hayden said to her as she walked toward the side gate that divided their houses.

She looked back at him. "What?"

"Let me know if you hear any more about Hector. I'm gonna have a couple of my guys tail him for a little while, just to be safe."

"Oh, Hayden. That's not necessary," she said.

"Yes, it is. See you around, Blake."

As she said goodbye and turned to leave, she jumped as she felt a hard slap on her ass. Instant stinging. She flew back around to see a grinning Hayden, looking proud.

"Sorry, couldn't help myself." He laughed as he walked back up his steps and violently swung the door open, disappearing inside.

Later that day, after she'd showered off the intoxicating Hayden scent, she sat down at her kitchen table to catch up on bills and responsibilities. She'd been dreading opening her unchecked phone all morning, afraid of the inevitable worried messages she'd have from Craig, since she never responded to his text the night before. But when she finally unlocked her phone, she saw only two messages from him. The first was sent a few hours after his first text, letting her know about dinner:

> *Craig: Hey babe, home from dinner. Man, those guys can drink. You're probably asleep already, but I just wanted to say goodnight and sweet dreams. Can't wait to see you on Sunday.*

The second text was sent that morning at 7 a.m.

> *Craig: Heading to another day of meetings. You ok? What's on your Saturday agenda?*

She quickly responded:

> *Blake: Hope meetings go well. I'm just headed out for a run (a lie) then maybe beach and shopping (also a lie)*

Craig: Have fun—don't spend too much {winky face emoji}

She laughed out loud at this.

At that exact moment, an SMS notification from her bank popped up on her phone.

Dear Mrs. Blake Davis,

This notification is to let you know you've exceeded your daily ATM withdrawal limit of $1200, at branch location 29348 in Ventura, CA. Your debit card will be frozen for 24 hours. If you believe this is an error, please reply to this message with CONTACT ME, and someone from our banking security department will call you soon. Wait times may vary. You can also contact us via your online banking app for faster service.

She stared at her phone. *What a weird spam alert.* Then all her blood rushed to her fingers and toes as she realized that it wasn't spam. Craig had her fucking debit card. Was he withdrawing her money? And was he in...Ventura? Not LA?

She immediately opened her banking app and saw her checking account balance had dropped more than two thousand dollars. Panicking, she clicked in to see the charges. The last three were ATM withdrawals all within a 30-mile radius of their house. The latest one was from that morning around the time Craig sent her that last text. He hadn't left town.

She sat there frozen at the kitchen table for several minutes, not sure what to do. Craig was clearly determined to ruin them financially. She needed to come up with a plan to save them, to save herself. She couldn't keep going on like this forever, pretending not to know about his secrets and lies. And frankly, she was tired of keeping her own secrets and telling her own lies. She needed to talk to Hayden again. He seemed to know all about this Hector, and she knew there was so much more that he wasn't telling her. Maybe Hayden could help her figure out how to get her husband out of this mess. Maybe after he was cleared of this gang affiliation and debt, then she would be free to confront him about Kendra and start moving toward a separation.

As she finalized her decision to talk to Hayden, she realized she didn't even have his phone number. She looked up from her table through the kitchen window and up at the house next door. *Guess I'll have to walk over there to talk to him.*

She dusted on a little make-up and changed into a cuter top before heading next door. But as she walked toward her front door, her sense of shame came rushing back, and she decided instead to take the backyard entrance. *Much more discreet.* After she climbed through the hole in the fence, she walked up the steps to the back door and knocked. No answer. *Shit, I forgot he said he had to go to a 'thing.'* She knocked again.

"Is anyone home?" she yelled loudly into the back window, hoping one of the other bikers would answer and she could at least get Hayden's phone number to text him. Crickets.

"Guess not," she said out loud.

"Is someone out there?" a man's voice called from somewhere behind her in the backyard. She jumped and turned around. No one was there.

"Hello?" she called out, timid.

"I'm in here!" the man's voice called back from somewhere

toward the edge of the backyard.

From the shed.

Chapter 9

Blake stood there, frozen.

"I'm in here!" the voice called again. "Come over here!"

The man in the shed was still alive.

Her eyes narrowed in on the voice and saw a hand poking out the back of the wooden slats, waving desperately, beckoning her.

Her legs unconsciously moved on their own, propelling her toward the giant shed. She had been obsessing over it since the day she witnessed the Army of Outlaws take the man prisoner and lock him up in there, fixated on knowing what and who was inside. In this moment, her obsession took over her body, and she found herself at the back wall of the shed, staring in horror at the rogue hand reaching for her. Like something out of a zombie movie.

She couldn't stop herself. She had to know who was inside.

"Who are you?" she asked the arm, her body buzzing with adrenaline.

"My name is Robert! I've been locked in here for...I don't know. A long time." His voice was desperate, almost pathetic.

"Are you...are you one of them?"

"No," she said quietly. "Just a neighbor."

"Oh, thank god," Robert said, visceral relief in his voice.

"You have to help me."

"I don't know…"

"Please!" he begged. "I'm almost out—I'm just…stuck. I just need a hand."

Fuck. Hayden and his friends could be gone for any number of hours. And Robert was going to escape, with or without her help. She thought about the consequences of interfering with this situation, about what Hayden's club might do to her if she helped this man. She shuddered to think what would happen if she were implicated. But he was basically already out…

Suddenly she was at the shed's front door. It was locked from the outside by a heavy, wooden bar wedged across the opening. She leaned into the door, using her body as leverage to move the heavy bar off its hinges. The wood made an abrasive scraping noise as she shoved it out of the way to unbarricade the door. She inhaled and exhaled deeply before opening the door.

As soon as the door opened, the smell hit her. Vomit, human feces, rotten food, urine. She gagged loudly, coughing into her hands.

"Back here!" Robert pleaded from the dark corner of the shed.

She looked around and realized she was standing inside what looked like a *Dexter* style kill room. The inside walls were lined with soundproofing material, and tarps were hung vertically in front of each wall. She looked under her feet and saw the floor was also lined with tarps. There was a utility cart pushed up against one of the walls, which contained plastic storage containers filled with tools and weapons. One container was stuffed with zip ties. Another had a varietal assortment of knives and blades. And one to the far edge of one of the shelves had what looked like Halloween costume material, which upon further inspection she realized was a box of masks. Other containers below held more unsettling items that she couldn't quite make out in the dark.

"Why did they lock you up?" she finally asked, tears welling up in her eyes from the smell. She tried to hold her breath.

"I have no idea. I don't know who these people are. All I know is they jumped me and locked me up in here. Please, you have to help me get out of here!"

She moved closer toward him, forcing herself to breathe through her mouth. In the corner by the man, she noticed a bucket with flies buzzing around it. *Ohmygod. Is that his toilet?*

"Are you hurt?" she asked, getting close enough to see him better. The sliver of light beaming in from the broken slat helped her eyes adjust. She couldn't make out his facial features, but she could see he was a gaunt, taller man. He was sitting on a bar stool with ropes hanging all around him.

"My wrist is broken," he said.

As she finally reached him, she could make out swelling and bruises on his face. There was dried blood all over his mouth and chin. His eyes looked bloodshot.

"You said you're almost free. You look tied up?"

"Hang on," the man said. He slid his right arm easily out of a knotted piece of rope and reached to the wall behind him, opening the broken slat further. He'd managed to cut a human-sized hole in the wall.

He then wiggled his feet out of their ropes to reveal that he had three out of four limbs completely free. Only his left arm was still bound tightly and securely, the only thing preventing him from escaping.

"I was able to get out of most of the binds, until my wrist broke." He looked up at her in desperation, and she could now see every detail of his face, backlit by the sunlight shining through. He looked like he was on the brink of death, red rings around his sunken eyes, his face concaved from malnutrition.

"Can you untie this hand for me?" He sucked in a breathy sob, motioning to the limp mess of bones in his free hand. "I was about to just push through the pain and do it myself until I heard you out there. I know it was a risk to call out to you, but I just somehow knew you weren't one of them."

She moved closer to him, inspecting the rope. The knot looked complicated, like it had been tied by someone with true binding expertise. Like a Boy Scout. Or a BDSM dom.

"Hang on. Let me look for a knife or something sharp to cut it loose."

"A knife would be better than how I managed to do it on the first hand," he said, showing her his teeth. His front tooth was chipped almost all the way to the gum.

"You *chewed* your way out?" she asked, horrified.

"I thought they were going to kill me," he said. "And now I know for sure that they are. Thank god you're here. You sweet, beautiful angel."

Now that there was light shining into the shed, she could get a better look at the torture chamber toolboxes in the corner. She spotted a box cutter and grabbed it. But as she turned around, she noticed a pair of handcuffs hanging on the wall behind the tools.

Instinct took over.

"How did you manage to cut a hole open in that wall?" she called over to him, motioning behind him.

He turned his head to meet her gaze at the hole.

She grabbed the handcuffs while he wasn't looking and shoved them in her jeans back pocket.

"That's how I broke my wrist," he said, turning back to face her. "Oh, thank god. You found a box cutter."

His voice was so meek, so gentle, that she felt bad for him. She walked back over to him, box cutter in hand. Eyeing the rope, she stepped behind him.

"I think I can get a better angle to cut it from back here," she said. She looked at his left hand that was still secured in the rope. Then her eyes wandered over to his right hand, which was now resting in a section of the rope, secured into a hangman's loop position with expert ties. It was how he'd been pretending to be tied up, by placing his hand inside the loop and then rolling his hand up into it to give the illusion of being bound. Her eyes scanned the rope up toward the ceiling, and she realized both the rope and its loop were secured. Only his hand was loose.

Without hesitating, she pulled the handcuffs from her back pocket and slammed one of them down on his wrist, forcing it shut, and then slammed the other onto the hangman's noose.

"What...what the fuck?" His voice was pure shock.

She backed away from him, realizing he was now securely restrained again. What was it that Hayden had said to her the day before? *Can't you just trust that he's where he deserves to be?* That sentence had been playing over and over in her mind as she realized that she knew Hayden better than she knew Hayden's prisoner, and Hayden so far had been true to his word. She had no reason not to trust him. But she had reason not to trust Robert.

"What have you done?!" he yelled, as he realized what was happening.

Blake walked backward toward the door where she'd entered, too afraid to turn her back on him, her hands shaking violently from the adrenaline and fear. She didn't answer him.

"YOU FUCKING BITCH! WHAT HAVE YOU DONE!" he screamed even louder. "I'LL FUCKING KILL YOU!"

Her back brushed up against the door and she realized she was at the exit of the shed. "I'm sorry," she finally said.

The thunderous sound of motorcycles filled the air behind her. She stumbled backward out of the shed, barely catching herself from falling as she made it back onto the grass in the backyard. She coughed and gagged violently as her lungs allowed her to breathe in through her nose again, and as the shock of the scene wore off, her nausea set in.

What felt like swarms of motorcycles zoomed into the backyard, and she was now aware of several men behind her.

"What the hell is going on here?" she heard Hayden's voice yell in her direction. "What are you doing here?"

She felt vomit rising inside of her and couldn't muster up the strength to respond. Hayden ran toward her and grabbed her by the shoulders, shaking her violently.

"What is going on?" he asked, looking into her eyes, his blue eyes burning with rage. "What did you do?"

She didn't answer. The other men got off their bikes and ran toward the shed, where the door was wide open. She heard Robert scream like a child, and then she heard loud, smacking noises, like someone being beaten. Robert was silent.

Dave emerged from the shed. "Hayden," he said, eyeing Blake cautiously as he addressed him. "Come look at this."

Hayden turned back to Blake.

"Get out of here now," he said to her. But she just stood there, staring blankly at him.

"I said get the *fuck* out of here, now!" Hayden yelled into her face, startling her out of her shocked state. Her eyes took in the sight around her, Hayden screaming in her face, with Dave, Elvis, Red, Rocco, and some other guy she didn't know at the entrance of the shed. All eyes on her. Her body woke up, and she turned around and ran toward the fence between their houses, climbing through the hole and continuing running without looking back until she was safely in her home with the doors locked.

Once she was inside, she burst into tears, her breath coming in hyperventilated sobs until she collapsed to the floor in her laundry room, burying her face in her hands and shaking violently as her body invited a physical response to what had just happened. She let the tears and shaking flow through her as she tightened her arms and legs into a little ball.

And then she heard it. A loud *pop*, like a firecracker.

Chapter 10

There was no mistaking it. Someone fired a gun next door. She stayed curled up in a ball on the laundry room floor, not sure what to do with herself. Was this what shock felt like?

She remained on the floor for what felt like hours, but her trance was suddenly broken by a knock at her back door. She stretched her neck to peer around the wall and saw Hayden on the other side of the glass. Willing herself to stand up, she made her way to the door, unlocking and opening it.

"Are you ok?" Hayden asked immediately.

She just stared at him and shrugged her shoulders. She couldn't form words yet.

"Can I come in?" he asked, looking over his shoulder at his own house. She opened the door wider, and he stepped inside.

"I know what you did," he said, facing her in her kitchen. "And I just want to say...thank you."

"Is he dead?" she finally asked, the first words out of her mouth since she'd spoken to Robert.

"Yes."

She opened her mouth to speak again but found she couldn't.

"Listen, Blake," he said, walking toward her to close the gap between them. "I want you to know you did the right thing. That man—"

"—Robert," she interrupted.

"Yeah. Robert. He was a bad man, ok?"

Was. He was already using the past tense to describe him. She felt the hair on her arms standing up.

"He's the reason for the wake you went to yesterday," he continued. "He murdered my friend Kelly. He raped her. Then he strangled her to death."

He looked into her eyes for a response. She just continued staring at him, fighting every urge to run and hide.

"My family and I...we don't involve the police in our business for obvious reasons. We take justice into our own hands. We held a trial for him this week and he was sentenced to execution...which wasn't supposed to happen until tomorrow. But since he tried to escape, we had to speed things up." He stopped again, giving her an opportunity to respond. Still, she said nothing. "Are you ok?" he asked again.

When she didn't respond, he said, "Guess that's a no," and pulled her into his arms to comfort her. She could smell his pheromones again, even sweatier than usual. She was instantly turned on, and that shocked her.

What is wrong with me? I just witnessed a murder and I'm thinking about...sex?

Before she could stop herself, she looked up into Hayden's eyes, placed her hand around the back of his head, and pulled his face into hers. She pressed her lips into his lips. He was still at first, seemingly confused by her behavior. But as she continued kissing him, he responded almost aggressively, kissing her back, forceful and passionate. His tattooed hands moved down to her waist, pulling her hips into him. She could feel that he was already hard. As they continued kissing, his hands explored her body, gliding one of them up her shirt and then under her bra. His calloused fingers were everywhere, and she felt ecstatic. She let her hands explore his body too, and as she reached the waist of his jeans, she felt something else big and hard sticking out of the back of his pants. A gun.

He lifted her by her waist effortlessly, and placed her onto the kitchen counter, just like the day before when he'd bandaged her up, except this time, his intentions were different. He pulled her shirt over her head and her bra cup down, kissing her nipple. She sighed softly. He then took his own shirt off, and she let her fingers explore his abs, which she'd been endlessly lusting after. They began unbuttoning each other's jeans as they kissed passionately.

"Your body is unreal," she said.

"So is yours, Blake. Those curves."

He lifted her butt off the counter, and with one smooth motion, pulled her jeans down to her ankles before setting her back down, her bare skin pressed against the cold marble countertop. Spreading her legs, he knelt in front of her and buried his face between them.

"Oh my god," she said, closing her eyes. "I can't believe this is happening."

After going down on her for several minutes and giving her an intense orgasm, he stood back up, unzipping his jeans. He pulled the gun out of the back of his waistband, and carefully set it on the counter. She felt alive and wild.

"You're so beautiful," he said, kissing her on the lips so she would taste herself on him. He pulled her hips toward him and then he was inside of her. Finally.

"So, what's going to happen to the body?" she asked Hayden a while later. They were splayed out on top of the white shag rug on her hardwood living room floor, their naked bodies intertwined like pretzels.

"That's the first thing you want to say to me after we have sex?" Hayden laughed, as he lightly traced his thumb along her shoulder and collarbone.

"Sorry, I think it's just now hitting me...what happened earlier. I've never heard anyone get murdered before."

"*Murder* is a strong word."

"Ok, I've never heard anyone get *executed* before."

"Don't you worry about a thing, sweetheart. It's all over now. My boys are taking care of it. I promise nothing bad will happen to you. Especially now that you've proven to my entire club that you can be trusted."

He tilted her chin towards him with his finger and pulled her in for a passionate kiss.

"Shit!" she yelled, pulling out of the embrace and jumping to her feet. "I just remembered."

"What?" Hayden looked alarmed.

"Shit shit shit!" she screamed, frantically searching for her clothes.

"Are you gonna make me guess?"

"I completely forgot. The whole reason I went to your house in the first place!"

"To see me?" He winked at her confidently. "Just couldn't get enough, I know."

"No, you asshole," she said more angrily than she intended, picking up his jeans and throwing them at him on the floor. "I was coming to tell you that Craig isn't really on a business trip in LA. He's here in town."

"How do you know?" he asked, standing up and stepping into his jeans. *God he's sexy.* She shuddered at this thought. *Stop that! Now is not the time!*

"Because he tried to withdraw all my money from my checking account at an ATM nearby, and I got an alert on my phone."

"So, he's still caught up in the mess with Hector," he said, shaking his head. "When is he coming back?"

"He wasn't supposed to be back until tomorrow, but now I don't know. He could be home at any time." She found his shirt and threw it at him. He caught it with ease. "So, you need to leave now!"

"Wow, I make love to you and you're throwing me out without even a cuddle?" he teased as he put his shirt on. "I hope you're at least planning on calling me again."

She was too stressed to laugh at his feigned clinginess. "Actually, I don't even have your phone number! That's why I went over to your house like that."

"Well, apparently not giving you my phone number was a blessing in disguise then, wasn't it? I had you to do my dirty work for me while I was gone."

"Too soon, Hayden," she said, shimmying into her jeans.

"Give me your phone then."

She walked over to the kitchen counter and grabbed her phone, unlocking it and placing it in Hayden's hand. After he put his phone number into her contacts, she heard his own phone buzz in his pocket.

"I just called myself from your phone, so now I have your number too," he said, handing the phone back to her. She looked at the new contact.

"Really? 'H Money'?"

"It's probably best that you don't have my real name in there," he said, smirking. "Catch you later, gorgeous."

He leaned in for one more kiss, and then left through the back door. Back to the active crime scene.

As she soaked in the bathtub that evening, she felt like she was crawling out of her own skin, like her organs and blood were trying to burst through their prison walls. The combination of fear, anxiety, post-traumatic stress, guilt, and sexual fulfillment both nauseated and excited her. She'd never felt this alive before, never had this sense of adventure.

But the image of Robert's swollen eyes and blood-caked lips as he screamed, "YOU FUCKING BITCH! I'LL FUCKING KILL YOU," kept flashing through her mind, and her heart would skip a beat each time the image came reeling back. Each vision would send a new surge of adrenaline through her. It somehow didn't feel real, like the aftermath of a vivid nightmare. She had to keep reminding herself that it was, in fact, real, that there really had been a man in that shed, that she'd looked him in the eye and spoken to him, and that she'd re-imprisoned him, effectively and directly contributing to his murder. But she didn't feel bad about it somehow. She felt righteous, like she'd played judge and jury and decided this bad man's fate.

She shifted around in the tub to stretch her legs all the way out to the faucet-side wall and closed her eyes.

And then there was Hayden. Beautiful, hot, hard Hayden. Everything about him screamed trouble, and yet she was drawn to him in this unexplainably chemical way. This strange thing between them was primal, sexually charged, *unpredictable*. She never knew what mood he'd be in or what he'd say or do next, and that thrilled her.

What was happening to her brain? She wasn't brought up to be an adrenaline junkie who broke the law and broke her vows. She was raised by educated, warm people who taught her to be compassionate and morally sound, to treat others with respect. Still, she'd grown into a wild child in her college years, which she'd worked to course correct in her mid-20s, forcing herself to grow up. And yet, in the short time she'd been living in California, all that moral fiber that had been woven into her over the past 32 years had come unraveled, reawakening something deep inside her: *an addiction to danger.*

Buzz, buzz.

A text alert on her phone.

Reaching for a towel, she hastily dried off a hand and grabbed her phone off the toilet seat. Jasmine. She swiped up to unlock it.

> *Jasmine: Hey girl, just checking in on you. Haven't heard back and am getting a little worried. Hope everything's ok.*

> *Blake: Hey! I'm so sorry for not responding. Didn't mean to worry you! Just been crazy busy!*

> *Jasmine: All good. Glad you're good.*

> *Blake: I miss you so much. You have no idea. Talk soon?*

> *She teared up as she sent the text to her friend.*

> *Jasmine: Aww I miss you too! I'm free this weekend for a phone date. Xoxo*

> *Blake: YASSS*

She set the phone down and laid back into the warmth of her bath, suddenly feeling more emotional about the day's events.

Hearing from Jasmine was a painful reminder of her old life, the life where she'd had a career and friends and a husband she loved, unlike her new life where she was isolated and spent her days either alone, with her cheating, lying husband, or in the company of a bike gang.

She was feeling sorry for herself when her phone buzzed again. Thinking it was Jasmine setting a time for their phone date, she took her time drying her hand and picking her phone back up again. But her breath caught in her throat when she saw that the notification was from H Money.

H Money: I can still taste you.

She bit her lip, heart racing, formulating a response in her head.

Blake: Dirty boy. Why don't you shower?

H Money: Because I like having all your juices on me

Blake: that's {fire emoji}

H Money: WYD sweetheart?

Blake smiled mischievously and snapped a photo of her legs in the bubbly water, then hit send.

H Money: Where's my invite?

Blake: Tiny bathtub {kissing emoji}

No response. She decided to send a follow-up.

Blake: Today was amazing. Is that terrible for me to say, given everything that happened?

H Money: Not terrible. I feel like maybe u r in shock though and haven't fully processed everything

Blake: I'm ok. {smiling emoji}

H Money: emoji queen {eggplant emoji} {water squirting emoji} {peach emoji}

Was he trying to *sext* her with emojis?

Blake: more like emoji {king emoji}

H Money: I'm worried about you over there in that house all alone, with bad men lurking. Want some company?

She felt an electric jolt as she read this latest text. She *did* want his company, badly. But she was also afraid of Craig coming home early, since he wasn't really in LA like he'd said. She'd already put her life at risk that afternoon and was afraid to do it again so soon.

Blake: Thank you. I'm really ok. We have good locks on the doors and windows here. I think I'm just gonna go to bed.

H Money: All good. I'll just be over here thinking about you in that bathtub.

Blake: {heart emoji}

When Hayden didn't respond, she figured the text exchange had ended and begrudgingly deleted the entire conversation from her phone. And as she came down from her adrenaline high, she laid back into her bath. It then occurred to her that she'd been so riled up from the events of that afternoon, that she hadn't had a sip of alcohol the entire day.

Chapter 11

She awoke Sunday morning to an empty house and a clear head. With a profound sense of living her most exciting life, she blasted her favorite Bastille album as she brewed coffee and danced around her kitchen in her pajama shorts. Feeling energized for the day, she wandered out into her backyard with her cup of coffee, wanting to check out the neighboring yard for the first time since The Execution. But when she stepped onto her back patio, she was startled to see something had changed.

The hole in the fence had been fixed.

For some reason, this change upset her. Why had they suddenly fixed the hole after the previous day's events? Had Hayden done it, or maybe instructed one of his club members to do it? Were they trying to keep her out of their yard? After she'd helped them, she thought she'd proven she could be trusted. And now they were shutting her out. She started to cry and was confused by this physical response. But as she thought more about it, sitting on the steps in her backyard, she realized why she was so upset. This club next door was the only good thing in her new life in California. If she no longer had them, she was left with the reality of her situation: her husband was having an affair, had gambled them into serious debt, had put their lives in danger, and she couldn't even be the blameless victim in all of it, which would have been a silver lining, giving her the pity and self-righteous card. She was at fault too. She'd slept with Hayden. Now they were both bad.

She needed to come up with a plan to deal with her situation with Craig. With the Army of Outlaws potentially cutting her off, she couldn't keep waiting around to deal with her marital problems. Wandering out into her backyard, she casually scanned the fence in between the two houses to see if there were any other holes to look through, but there were none. She could, however, see over the top of the fence, but not all the way into the backyard. She sighed and looked up at her orange tree, jumping up to pull a low hanging one from its branch. It snapped off easily, sending the branch flying upward, and she stepped backward to avoid getting smacked. Brushing off the orange in her hand, she willed herself to think through how to deal with everything.

On the one hand, *she* wasn't the one in trouble with Hector. If she really wanted to escape, she could go back to Arizona and crash with Jasmine until she got back on her feet, and she could leave Craig in California to deal with his own mess without anyone coming after her. But her savings were tied to his, and there was a possibility Hector could take all her money too. And if she was really being honest with herself, she wasn't prepared to leave Hayden yet. Something about this motorcycle club captivated her and made her feel truly alive in a way she'd never felt before, and she craved more of it. She wanted them to accept her, to let her back in.

Ok, I think I need to see this thing through. I need to find a way to solve the Hector problem and protect my assets before I deal with confronting Craig. Once Hector is dealt with, I will tell Craig I know everything, and I'll take him for everything he's got.

She felt relieved to have a plan in place.

After returning to her kitchen, she washed the orange under the faucet and then ate it over the sink voraciously, like a barbarian. She was wiping the juice from her chin with the back of her hand when she heard the front door unlocking.

Craig opened the door and emerged in the doorway. One of his arms was in a sling. His face was swollen and purple, his eyes black and blue, like he'd been "mugged" again.

"Craig!" she yelled, sincerely, as she ran over to meet him in the front entryway.

"Don't worry," he was already saying before she'd finished saying his name. "It looks way worse than it is. I was in a car accident with Bill."

"What?!" she demanded, exasperated.

"Yeah, we were in his car this morning after checking out of our hotel, when a truck T-boned us at an intersection."

Craig continued with his story while Blake pretended to believe him and walked to the laundry room to retrieve the first aid kit. She touched the handle on the kit and Hayden's face flashed in her memory, sending tingles down her body as she remembered him opening the same kit to bandage up her legs only two days before. Shaking off the exciting memory and reanimating her concerned look, she walked back into the living room to play nurse to her husband.

"And so, we were in and out of that ER, and they sent us home so quickly, that I didn't want to worry you by calling you," he was finishing his story. "Well mostly Bill didn't want to worry Sarah, and I was following his lead."

She sat down next to him on the couch and studied his battered face. He no longer looked handsome to her, and it wasn't just that everything was swollen and bruised. It was

119

that she now saw him for what he truly was when she looked into his eyes: a selfish, narcissistic liar. If he was capable of really loving her, he wouldn't have endangered their lives, put them into financial ruin, and certainly not had an affair with some young bimbo. But she had to play this very carefully, and not arouse any suspicion that she knew about his double life.

She left him alone the rest of the afternoon, giving him space to shower and settle in.

"Let's order delivery tonight," she said that evening, placing a hand on Craig's shoulder from behind the couch while he was watching the news.

When he didn't respond, she looked up to meet his point of focus on the TV. The local news was covering a missing woman. A missing woman named Kendra Johnson.

Kendra.

A missing person flyer flashed on the screen while a reporter covered the story. In the photo was a beautiful woman with dark hair. There was no doubt in her mind. It was Craig's Kendra.

She looked down at her husband's face and studied his expression. It was blank, distant, his feelings buried deep down inside. He was motionless and speechless. His t-shirt where her hand rested on his shoulder felt damp with sweat. His eyes were locked on the TV.

"Twenty-six-year-old Kendra Johnson was last seen Friday evening leaving the hospital where she works as a nurse in the maternity ward. Her car was found parked in the hospital employees' lot the following morning after she failed to report to work, and her family had not heard from her. While there is very little information so far, police believe there was no reason for Kendra to take off without telling her loved ones, and foul play has not been ruled out. Police, as well as Kendra's family, are urging anyone with information to come forward. Her family and friends will be holding a vigil tonight, and forming a search party for the surrounding area tomorrow..."

The scene cut to an older, attractive woman.

"We just want our baby to come home," the woman, Blake assumed to be Kendra's mother, pleaded through tears. "She's a hard-working, young nurse who cares deeply for others, has so many dear friends, and spends her free time volunteering in the community. She's planning to attend medical school in the fall. She is loved by so many..."

So, Blake thought dryly, *I guess she's not a bimbo.*

She looked down at Craig's face again. He was still staring at the TV screen, not speaking. Lifting her hand off his shoulder, she slowly backed away.

"I'm sorry, sweetie," he said suddenly, his trance broken. "Did you say something?"

"Nothing important," she said. Then, carefully, "That's really sad about that girl."

"Yeah."

"Hopefully she's ok." She kept her voice calm and collected while burning thoughts raged through her mind. *You probably know if she's ok, don't you? Oh, Craig. What did you do?*

"We'll see, I guess."

They were silent for a moment, clearly neither of them knowing what to say next.

Then there was a deafening, crashing sound that startled them both, sending them jumping several feet across the room.

Blake screamed, ducking behind the couch.

Something had been thrown through their front living room window, shattering the glass all over their entryway. She scanned the room to see what had broken the window and saw a large grey rock on the floor of the kitchen, a trail of glass shards leading up to it like breadcrumbs.

"What in the actual fuck?!" Craig yelled, shielding his wife from the stray pieces of broken glass.

Craig rushed over to the rock and picked it up with his non-sling-bound hand. As Blake stood from her crouching position, she could see there were flames drawn on one side of the rock in red paint. Or was that...*blood*?

Fire... *Don't play with fire.*

Hector's text to Craig on the burner phone. She'd mentioned it to Hayden, and he flinched at those words. This rock had to be Hector's doing.

"Are you ok?" Craig asked her, becoming more aware of the situation in front of him. He set the rock on the kitchen counter and walked toward her with his now free hand outstretched toward her, like he was going to pet her.

"I'm fine," she said, unconsciously taking a step back. "Are *you* ok?"

"Fine." He looked over to their front window, fear in his eyes.

"Should we call the police?" she asked.

"Of course," he replied, not very convincingly. "But...I don't want to deal with all that tonight. It will take hours and it's already been an exhausting day. You stay here where it's safe. I'm just gonna do a lap outside to make sure whoever it was that threw this is gone now. Then I guess I'll just have to secure the house and board up the window tonight, and we can deal with this all in the morning."

Blake looked at him apprehensively, her body still shaking.

"I'm sure it was just some punk teenagers playing a prank," he said reassuringly. "You know how this neighborhood is."

"Ok," she said, walking toward the kitchen windows. "But let me help you lock everything up. You only have one working arm."

Neither of them slept for hours after they went to bed that night. She was wired with adrenaline and fear, and she could feel Craig tossing and turning beside her.

Finally, when Craig lay still for a while, and enough time had passed that she was sure he was asleep, she silently rolled out of bed and wandered into the kitchen. Everything was still, seemingly safe. They'd patched up the front window with some plywood and sealed it shut until it could be replaced, but she still felt unsettled. Why did Hector throw a rock through their window? It was clearly a warning, but for what? Was her life in danger?

She looked at the clock. It was only midnight. Maybe Hayden was still awake. Too afraid to text him with her husband in the house, she slowly pulled back the curtain to see if any lights were on next door.

Sure enough, Hayden's bedroom light was on. She stared into the window for several seconds, but no one appeared. Then, shifting her gaze to the front entrance of their house, she saw a woman locking her car and walking up their driveway, carrying a duffle bag. As the woman neared the house and the light from their front porch shone onto her face, Blake recognized her. It was the dark-haired girl. Christina.

She watched as Christina waited at the front door, duffle bag in tow, to be let in. Finally, the door swung open. Hayden stood there, shirtless.

"Come on in, sweetheart," Blake saw him mouth to her. Christina slipped inside.

She didn't wait around to see if Hayden's bedroom light

would turn off, or what would happen next. But she felt nauseous.

Chapter 12

In the morning, she awoke to Craig setting a hot cup of coffee on the bedside table next to her head. As she slowly opened her eyes, she saw he was in gym shorts and a ratty old t-shirt.

"What's this for?" she asked sleepily, sitting up in bed to drink her coffee.

"Called in sick today so I can deal with this mess." He pointed toward the other side of the house, beyond their bedroom wall, where the rock had landed. "I figure since I was in an accident yesterday while on work time, I should be fine to take today off."

"Of course," she agreed. "Have you called the police yet about the rock?"

"Yes, just a few minutes ago," he said, walking to the closet to grab a sweatshirt and pull it over his head. "They're coming over later this morning to file a report."

"Oh good."

"Listen," he said, turning back to face her. "Why don't you get out of here and enjoy your day, babe? I don't want you to have to deal with this. Let me take care of it."

Was he kicking her out? Why didn't he want her there?

"Actually, would you mind picking up a few things from the hardware store? The installation guy is coming over later this week to fix the broken window, so I've been YouTubing how to create a temporary fix, and I have almost everything I need to do it. Just need a couple things if you don't mind running out to get them for me?"

"Sure, no problem," she said, pulling back the covers and getting out of bed. Was this for real, or was he playing her? "Let me just get showered, and then I'll head out."

"Great. I'll make a list."

As she got ready in her bathroom, she heard Craig wander out to the garage to rummage through his tools. Since he was distracted, she decided to curl her hair into soft beach waves and put on a little more make up than her normal "day" look, giving herself a smoky eye and pop of color on her lips. She went to her closet and selected a suggestively short, white lace dress that was cut just low enough to highlight the top curves of her breasts. She usually wore this as a swimsuit cover up, but decided it was a hot enough day that she could rock it over regular underwear, pairing it with her Steve Madden nude strappy heels.

As she grabbed her purse and keys from the kitchen, she zoomed past the garage door so that Craig wouldn't take notice of her appearance, and instead called to him from the front door.

"Be back later!"

"Thanks for running that errand," he called back. "Take your time! I've got everything under control here."

I'll bet you do.

She pulled her car into the hardware store parking lot and parked in the shade. Then, impulsively picking up her phone, she selected H Money from her contacts and pulled up a new, blank text box.

Blake: Busy?

H Money (responding almost immediately): Not too busy for you, sweetheart. What's up?

Blake: Can we meet somewhere and talk?

H Money: I'm at Cold Spring Tavern. Roll over.

Blake: Cool, be there soon.

Heart racing, Blake embraced this new exhilarating feeling she now craved. She turned off her car and went into the hardware store to purchase the items Craig had requested. Once she was done with her errand, she plugged Cold Spring Tavern into her phone. It was located up in the hills beyond Santa Barbara, about 40 minutes away. She pressed GO on the navigation and headed to meet Hayden.

As she pulled up to the location, she was surprised to see that it was a charming row of little cottages, nestled into the forest like a scene out of a children's storybook. Lush trees surrounded the cottages on all sides, except for a paved road that passed along the front of it. Upon further inspection, she realized it was a biker hangout, despite the cozy Hansel and Gretel architecture. There were at least a dozen motorcycles parked out front, and the people walking around outside looked hard: men with chops and other extreme facial hair, men wearing cuts and flicking lit cigarettes into the bushes, small groups drinking their beers out in the side alley, women in corsets with cross necklaces wedged into their pushed-up cleavage. There was a band of three older men with long beards playing live country music out front of one of the cottages, while bikers swayed along to the banjo and mediocre singing as they drank their beers and ate their freshly BBQed tri tip sandwiches. The scene reminded her of the wake Hayden had taken her to. She unquestionably was going to stand out in her little white hippie dress but found she didn't care anymore.

I am different from them. Who wants to blend in when you can turn heads?

The adrenaline of what she was about to do gave her that extra boost of confidence she needed to exit her car and walk toward the cottage with the "TAVERN" sign.

Just as she suspected, all heads and eyes were on her as she strutted through the western style bar doors in her little white dress, and entered the dark, dank dive. She looked around for Hayden but didn't immediately see him. Not wanting to lose her confidence-infused momentum, she walked directly toward an open stool at the bar and sat down. The bar was packed with bikers and their groupies, playing pool, drinking, threatening each other. No one was trying to hide the fact that they had their eyes on her. Blake didn't recognize any of them.

A tattooed woman in a too-tight tank top behind the bar walked toward her. She had a septum piercing in her nose, and her chest cleavage was weathered and wrinkled from the sun, like leather.

"What can I get for ya, honey?" she asked in a smoky voice.

"Vodka soda, please," she answered automatically.

"Any preference on vodka?"

"Tito's, if you have it."

"I didn't peg you for a basic bitch," a voice said behind her. Then, hands were around her neck and shoulders and she felt herself being swiveled around in her stool. She now faced

Hayden, who had her in a play headlock.

"I'll have you know that Tito's is a great value," she said in defense, prying his hands off her. "High quality, reasonable price." She crossed her arms.

"That's some dress," he said, hungrily eyeing her body. "Do you have anything on underneath it?" He gently lifted the skirt up her leg.

"That's none of your business," she responded playfully, batting away his prying hands.

"Ah that's right," he said, backing away and putting both hands in the air like a good boy. "You came here to *talk*."

"Yeah," she said.

"Well in that case," he said, turning to the old, seemingly drunk man on the stool next to her. "Yo, George!" He slapped the old man on the shoulder, which made George jump in his seat. "Mind if I sit next to this pretty lady?"

The old man looked judgingly at Blake, and then turned to Hayden as he hobbled off the stool. He mumbled something but Blake couldn't make it out. Hayden took the old man's place, swiveling Blake's stool by her bare legs to face him.

"Oh, thanks, Starla sweetheart," he said over Blake's shoulder to the leathery bartender, who had brought over Blake's vodka soda. "Go ahead and put this fine lady's drinks on my tab."

"You got it, Hayden," the bartender, Starla, replied obediently.

"Thanks for the drink," Blake said, taking a sip of the stiff vodka. Hayden sipped his own brown cocktail, while looking into her eyes with his trademark intensity.

"So, what's up, lady?"

"Hayden, there you are!" a familiar voice called over her

head. "You owe me $50. Elvis's old lady beat his ass for cheating on her again. He has a black eye today."

Blake turned around to see Dave standing there, looking excited.

"Oh, hey, neighbor," Dave said, suddenly noticing her.

"Hey."

"Hey, man, we're kind of in the middle of something," Hayden said to Dave.

"You want to place another bet?" Dave challenged, his voice slightly slurred. "Scorned old ladies are so goddammed predictable, it's ridiculous."

Hayden opened his mouth to say something but was interrupted by a man in an Army of Outlaws cut standing up from a table behind Dave. *Rocco.* His bald head was shiny as ever, an extreme contrast to his long, scraggly beard. Looking agitated, Rocco walked toward their group and placed a hand on Dave's shoulder. Dave's mood instantly changed.

"Keep your shit in check," Rocco said to Dave, authority in his voice. "Don't make me pull rank."

Dave slid out of Rocco's grasp. "I got it, man," he said, waving his hand dismissively. "I'm cool."

"Good," Rocco said, turning his focus to Blake. He glared at her with his beady eyes, judging her for trespassing into their world. "Enjoy your drinks."

Rocco turned away from them and returned to his table with other men in Army of Outlaws cuts.

"Maybe you should go try to hook up with one of those girls over there," Hayden said to Dave, cutting the tension. He pointed to a group of intimidating-looking women. "Instead of always being up on my dick."

Hayden pantomimed grabbing his own bulge as he teased

130

his friend, which Blake found both vulgar and hot at the same time.

"Go fuck yourself, man," Dave shot back at Hayden, his eyes threatening. He was clearly unnerved. But then he broke into affected laughter. "I'm just playin'. Good call about those chicks." He wandered away from them to go, she assumed, strike out with those women.

"Sorry about my friends," Hayden said to her. "I know they're a lot."

"I actually enjoy most of them," she said. *Other than Rocco. That guy hates me.* "If it weren't for them, I would have been on my own at that funeral."

"Well, it will be too hard to walk away from you now when you're in this dress." He pulled at the lace on her skirt, clearly hungry for her.

She batted him away again, still playing coy. Though she doubted anyone she knew would be in this bar, she still wanted to maintain a low profile. She sipped her drink through an awkward silence.

"So," she blurted, finally breaking it. "I noticed the fence is fixed."

Hayden looked uncomfortable, taking a swig of his own drink. "Yeah. For security."

"To keep your female neighbors out of your yard?" she asked playfully.

"To keep murderers out of yours."

"Oh," she said, embarrassed. "I guess that makes sense."

"Why do you look so disappointed?" Hayden was smiling now, enjoying her interest.

"Well..." she said, finishing her drink. "Now, what am I supposed to do for my nightly entertainment?"

Hayden silently signaled to Starla that they needed another round. Another vodka soda was in her hands within seconds.

"Neighbor!" Hayden laughed in his best *how dare you* voice. "Are you spying on me?"

"Never intentionally," she said, sipping her new cocktail. "You guys just make so much noise having people over at all hours of the night, it's hard not to notice. Like last night for example."

"What about last night?" He was swirling his whiskey in his glass.

"Your midnight booty call."

"My what?" He looked confused. "Oh, you mean Christina? She's staying at the house for a bit."

He wasn't denying sleeping with her but wasn't confirming it either. She continued sipping her drink.

"Am I sensing a little bit of...jealousy?" he asked, smiling bigger.

"Me? Never." She laughed confidently.

"Do I need to remind you that you're married and have a *husband*?" He playfully kicked at her barstool, swiveling her around in a circle. "I'm not looking to be your side piece. I've got more self-respect than that."

"I'm not jealous. I was just curious," she lied.

"I think about you a lot, Blake," he said, suddenly serious.

"I think about you too." Their faces were just inches from each other, their voices lowered now beneath the hum of the bar crowd.

He sat back. "Good." With that, he shot back the rest of his drink, swallowing every last drop. "So why are you here?"

"Ugh," she groaned. "So much is happening."

"Tell Daddy all about it."

She told him about the rock with painted flames thrown through their window the night before, and about Kendra-The-Mistress going missing. Hayden was silent through all of it, and by the time she finished the story he seemed sobered up.

"What should I do?" She placed a hand on his forearm.

He studied her for a moment, silent. And then his blue eyes became fiery, and he leaned in and placed his tattooed hand around her throat, pulling her into him and kissing her hard on the lips. She melted into his forceful grasp. She could feel eyes on them, but she no longer cared. His free hand grazed her thigh and glided upward, and now his fingers were reaching under her dress. He pulled his face back and looked into her eyes, searching for permission. She leaned forward into him and kissed him back, a silent yes. His hand continued exploring under her dress, and then his fingers were lightly touching the outside of her panties, tantalizing her.

"You should let me fuck you in the bathroom."

She was stunned. She hadn't expected this. She wasn't usually into sex in public restrooms. She could barely do her actual business in them, often performing the awkward hover-squat over the toilet seat to avoid touching any germs. But right then, in this dimly lit dive bar with loud country music playing in the background, lowered inhibitions floating around their atmosphere, and two stiff cocktails warming her insides, she nodded her head yes before allowing herself to analyze the situation.

Hayden stood up from his stool and held his hand out to help her up. Once they were both standing, he whispered into her ear, "I'll give you a head start."

She turned away from him and strutted toward the neon restroom sign. She didn't look back to see when or if Hayden would follow her. When she reached the dark hallway in the back, she let herself into the single-use women's restroom. She didn't lock it behind her. Walking over to the sink, she quickly fluffed her hair and did a teeth check in the mirror. The anticipation was exhilarating. As she stared at herself in the mirror, she studied her facial features. She'd always been told she was beautiful, ever since she was a little girl. Her blonde hair had always come in full and naturally wavy, but never frizzy. Her hazel eyes were bigger than average, with long, full lashes. She'd often been called "doe-eyed" by friends and family. Her lips, which were naturally full, looked extra plump today from her Kat Von D lip stain. She felt sexier than ever before.

Hayden opened the door and entered the bathroom. She didn't turn around but met his eyes through the mirror. He locked the door behind him and walked toward her.

She bit her lip in anticipation as he closed the gap between them, locking eyes with her in the mirror, grabbing her hard by the waist.

"Bend over," he ordered.

She did as she was told and leaned forward over the sink, arching her back so her butt pressed into the front of his jeans. He lifted her dress and gently pulled her panties to the side, licking his lips while he did so. Then she heard him unzipping his jeans, and within seconds he was inside of her, forcefully taking her from behind. She closed her eyes in ecstasy and felt him taking complete possession of her. She belonged to him. She was his to use. He grabbed her ass hard as they both came violently together.

Her legs were shaking as she stood up straight, and Hayden was kissing her neck sweetly.

"Sorry, I couldn't help myself," he whispered into her ear. "I blame the dress."

"I'm not complaining." She smiled with her eyes closed, out of breath.

"Let's get out of here," he suggested as he zipped his jeans back up. "Or do you have to get home?"

She dug into her purse and tapped her phone to see the time. "I don't have to get back just yet."

"Good," he said, walking toward the door. "I have somewhere I want to take you."

He exited the bathroom, and she locked the door behind him. Reaching back into her purse, she pulled out some powder and lipstick for a quick touch-up.

He better not be taking me to another funeral.

When she reemerged into the dark, dank ambiance, she spotted Hayden at the bar where they'd been sitting. He was closing the tab. As she approached him, he turned his back to her and walked over to Dave, muttering something quietly to him. Whatever Hayden told him seemed to sober him up and his silly demeanor turned serious. They both nodded and gave each other a bro-handshake-hug. Then Hayden turned to face her.

"You ready?"

"Where are we going?"

"Somewhere that I think you should see."

"Do you always have to do the whole mysterious thing?" she asked, rolling her eyes.

"You like it."

He took her hand and weaved her through the intimidating crowd. When they swung through the saloon doors, she was momentarily blinded by the bright light. She'd forgotten it was

135

still daytime.

"Let's take your car," he said, motioning to her high heels and dress.

"Oh," she said, surprised. She was suddenly filled with anxiety about going on another mystery adventure with Hayden but liked the idea of being in control of the vehicle used for the adventure. She nodded in hesitant agreement and pointed to her black Mazda. He grabbed a backpack out of his motorcycle storage, and as they walked toward the car, Hayden took her car keys out of her hand.

"Oh, I'm driving," he said confidently.

"Excuse me?"

"You weigh like nothing, and I just boozed you up," he said, smiling and penetrating her with his wicked eyes. "Plus, I like to be in control."

"Fine," she said, her heart fluttering. She felt conflicted that Hayden's controlling nature turned her on. Every book on feminism would tell her to punch him in the face and explain equal rights to him, but this felt different. Hayden didn't come from her modern world. There was something primal, almost cavemanlike, about his lifestyle. Hunter versus gatherer.

As they drove away from the row of cottages in the woods, her nerves set in. She knew she could hold her own around his biker friends, but she didn't like being blind-sided. She wanted to know what she was getting herself Into.

After about 45 minutes, they exited the freeway and made a left turn into an unfamiliar area, clearly headed into a less savory neighborhood. While living on The Avenue wasn't exactly the nice part of town, it was still relatively close to all the upscale beachfront property that warranted their property taxes to be so high. This new area felt more threatening. They drove down a residential street, where she saw clusters of men standing around on their porches drinking out of brown-bag-concealed beverages. As they turned onto a more commercial-looking block with office buildings and storefronts, Hayden sped up.

Blake opened her mouth to speak, then changed her mind and closed it. She did this several times. Hayden was annoyingly quiet, and she hated awkward silences. But she also didn't want him to think she was the kind of woman who needed to talk just to fill the space. There was so much to say and yet she was at a loss for words. Every time she felt the urge to speak, she caught herself preparing to comment on the weather or something else trivial, so she decided not speaking was a better option.

They pulled into an industrial business park filled with warehouses, and Hayden drove with intention toward a row of buildings in the back of the lot. As they slowed down, she saw a sign that said LOMPOC CONSTRUCTION. She'd heard of Lompoc, located in the northeast part of Santa Barbara County, adjacent to endless beautiful wine country. One of the women in her yoga class referred to it as "*Lompton*," a combination of "Lompoc" and "Compton," alluding to the high crime rate. But how bad could a city in Santa Barbara County really be?

"Want to tell me where we're going yet?" she finally asked, feeling this was an ok way to break the silence.

"To see what your husband's gotten himself into," Hayden replied, pulling down an alleyway and parking the car between a couple of nondescript vehicles.

"Meaning?"

"We're gonna check out the place where all your money's been spent."

Hayden got out of the car and opened the back driver's-side

137

door. He took off his precious Army of Outlaws cut, folded it gently and laid it in the backseat. Then he unzipped his backpack, pulled out a lightweight, grey zip-up hoodie and slid into it.

Going incognito. Fuck. We're going to Hector's casino.

"What if Craig is there right now?" Blake asked, horrified at the thought of busting her husband at his secret spot, biker date in tow.

"Woman, you need to learn to trust me. I've got eyes everywhere. Your husband is at home."

She nodded and gulped more audibly than she meant to. As they exited the car, she took two deep breaths secretly behind the passenger-side door to prepare herself.

Hayden took her hand, latching onto it as he directed her back down the alley toward the warehouses, and up to a large, white building. After looking both ways over his shoulder, he knocked on the front door.

A voice behind the door asked, "We're closed. Who's there?"

"I have a delivery for Mark," Hayden replied.

The industrial barn-style door slid open slightly, and a tan, Hispanic man poked his face out of the shadows.

"You got cash?"

Hayden must have anticipated this, because he immediately slipped his hand through the narrow opening and placed a gleaming stack of bills into the man's hand.

He's been here before.

The man slammed the door shut in Hayden's face, and Blake worried he'd made a mistake or had been ripped off. But after a few seconds, the door opened again, this time wide enough for the two of them to enter.

Once inside, Blake's eyes adjusted to the dimly lit interior. All the windows were boarded up so no natural light could intrude. There was one set of fluorescents in the corner, but they were flickering and buzzing angrily, only casting light over a small part of the room. In the far back corner, she could make out a stairwell behind some shelving with boxes. Standing next to the stairwell were two more intimidating men, and she caught a glimpse of a gun sticking out of one of their back pockets. She wondered if this was some sort of cliché speakeasy, where the casino was hidden underneath the unmarked warehouse, guarded by multiple men.

"Follow me," the doorman said, interrupting her thoughts. She studied him more closely now that she could see him better. He was short, maybe only a couple inches taller than her, but muscular and built. His bulging biceps were on the verge of ripping his t-shirt sleeves.

Hayden placed his fist gently into her back and nudged her forward, signaling for her to follow the overly jacked doorman. In her peripheral vision, she saw Hayden casually throw his hood over his head.

As she'd suspected, the doorman led them toward the barely hidden stairwell toward the back of the warehouse. The two men standing guard of the stairwell were silent as they passed through, not making eye contact with either of them. They began their descent into the dark unknown below, and a flickering thought invaded her brain. *You're never coming back up these stairs again, you dumb, dumb girl.*

Blake and Hayden emerged at the bottom of the stairs into another dimly lit room with yet another door. Except now, she could hear the muffled hum of a party behind this new threshold. *So, it is a speakeasy.*

The doorman punched a code into a lockbox next to the

seemingly final entrance, and the door slowly opened automatically for them. Instantly, she was hit with the stench of stale cigarettes and beer. Spanish-language rap music filled the air and set a nightclub-like tone to the abrasive neon signs lighting up the otherwise dark, anonymous room. It was easy to be incognito here. Everyone looked vaguely unremarkable in the light, which exposed only subtle hints of gender and ethnicity. She now understood why Hayden's half-assed attempt to disguise himself would be successful here.

The space was much larger than she'd anticipated, and she couldn't make out where the room ended, with the irritating reflection of the neon signs obstructing her view. Probably intentionally. There were what seemed like endless tables stationed around the room, some for poker, some for craps, some for other types of betting games she didn't recognize. Everyone seemed focused on themselves, not paying much attention to newcomers entering the casino. *Minding their own business.*

Hayden took the lead as they navigated through several tables without even so much as a glance in their direction. He led them to a blackjack table at one of the far corners of the room, which backed up into a dark, narrow hallway with more mystery doors. He steered her toward two empty seats at the table and turned to her.

"You know how to play?"

"A little."

"Good." He pulled one of the empty chairs back, motioning for her to sit. The pleather seat was sticky against her bare thighs, but she did her best to look comfortable, like she belonged. Hayden sat down to the left beside her and made a hand gesture to the dealer. Then, reaching into his pocket, he pulled out a handful of poker chips, placing a small stack in front of each of their spots at the table.

"How do you just magically have chips?" Blake whispered to Hayden.

"Always prepared, baby," he replied arrogantly, interlacing his fingers, and stretching his arms out in front of him, relaxed, or at least feigning relaxation. His hood really did obscure his identity.

The dealer was a tall, skinny, Hispanic boy with acne so bad that Blake could see it even in this strange pseudo-lit darkness. He looked no more than 16 or 17. After eyeing them with his best authoritative look, he dealt them into the game. She settled in, allowing herself to steal an inconspicuous glance at the people to the left and right of them. On her immediate right sat an older man with a mustache and cowboy hat. He smelled like unwashed clothes and cigar ashes and was hunched forward, focused only on the game. To the left of Hayden, there was another man in a baseball hat, appearing closer in age to them, although it was hard to make out in the darkness. She tried to play it cool and not stare, but there was something familiar about his facial features. The dealer started the game, and when she heard the baseball-capped man to the left of Hayden mutter, "hit," his voice sounded familiar too. Where did she know him from?

After a few minutes, a cocktail waitress in a too-tight dress appeared at their table to take their order. She looked young, no more than 20, but somehow like she'd already lived 40 years. The bags under her eyes accentuated by the neon lights suggested either a severe lack of sleep or a drug problem, and as Blake scanned the girl's nightgown of a dress hanging off her rail-thin body, she wagered it was probably drugs. The girl scowled at them overtly as she reluctantly took their orders before walking away from the table. Blake turned to Hayden and whispered into his ear.

"Remind me again what that this has to do with finding out about what Craig's been up to?"

"See those guys at the roulette table over there—three o'clock?" he responded without looking up from their own table, signaling with his hand to "stay" to the dealer.

She casually let her eyes wander to where Hayden directed her and saw a group of guys in leather cuts huddled around one of the tables.

"Those are Desperados," he whispered under the thudding base of the rap music, so only she could hear him. "I've had a tail on them, and it seems like your hubs is in tighter with them than I thought. We're here to do some recon."

She nodded her head and sipped the disgusting vodka soda that had appeared in front of her. She signaled "hit" to the dealer, and immediately busted. Hayden didn't pass her any more chips, but he was still in the game.

She was suddenly aware of her full bladder and turned to Hayden to say she was going to find a ladies' room. He pointed her in the direction of the restrooms, but as she stood up from the table, he grabbed her hard by the wrist, yanking her toward him.

"Don't talk to anyone," he warned her.

"I'm not stupid." She wiggled out of his grip and walked casually toward the bathrooms, which weren't hard to miss, since they were also lit up with neon signs. She entered the door under the *WOMEN* sign and walked into a halfway clean stall to pee. Hovering above the toilet, she saw that graffiti covered the entire stall door. There were etchings of fire and flames and some Spanish phrases, some of which she could translate from her days of Spanish classes in school. One stood out to her:

Las perras traidoras se queman

Traitor bitches get burned

Well, that's fucking ominous. She stood up and unlatched the stall door, walking toward the sinks to wash her hands. Bending down and tilting her head to pump the soap dispenser, she became aware of someone behind her. She looked up into the mirror.

The baseball-capped man from their table was behind her.

"Don't scream."

Chapter 13

Blake flipped around to face the man cornering her in the bathroom. Though frozen with fear, the irony of this being the second time a man had met her in a public bathroom that day was not lost on her.

"I'm not going to hurt you," the man said to Blake, recognizing the fear in her eyes. "Do you remember me?"

She studied his face for a sign of familiarity. Under the shadow of his baseball hat, she could see his eyes were dark and slightly sunken but encased in full lashes that made them sort of pretty. He was too thin, but something about his hollowed, angular cheekbones and jawline appealed to her.

"We met a few weeks ago," he said, gentler, clearly aware he'd spooked her. "At your house."

She searched her brain. *The detective!* What the hell was he doing at this underground casino? *Is he undercover?*

"You're the detective who came by my house that day," she said calmly, hoping to disguise her panic. "What was your name again?"

"Detective Vasquez."

"Ah, right."

"And you're...?"

"Blake."

"Blake," he said sternly as he inched toward her. "When I saw you in there and recognized you, I was deeply concerned. Are you in trouble?"

"What do you mean?" she played dumb.

"I'm so sorry for cornering you like this, but I didn't know how else to check on you without anyone else hearing." He glanced behind him at the bathroom entrance door, which was locked, apparently by him when he barged in to confront her. "This isn't how we normally do things."

"We?"

"Police. We're not supposed to scare innocent citizens in restrooms at seedy underground casinos."

"You didn't scare me."

"Either way," he said, shaking his head. "I shouldn't have snuck up on you. Are you ok?"

"Yes, I'm ok."

"Why are you here?"

She panicked and went with instinct. "Why are *you* here?"

He raised his eyebrows. "Official business."

She gestured to his street clothes. He smirked and said, "Blending in."

"Am I in trouble for something? I didn't even know what this place was before I got here."

"If I were here to arrest people, please believe me that you'd be far down on the list," he said, smiling. "I've got bigger thugs to fry."

"Ok, well I was just getting ready to leave," she said, eyeing the door.

"Do you have any idea who you're dealing with?" he asked, realizing he wasn't getting through to her.

"Who do you mean?" She was clutching her purse tightly.

"You're getting involved with bike gangs. Do you know how dangerous that is for someone like you?"

"Someone like *what*?" She was defensive.

"A nice, normal suburban girl," he replied. "Girls like you have a tendency to end up missing when mixing with men like them. I'm worried for your safety."

She thought about Kendra. Kendra who was missing. She didn't want to end up like her. She didn't want to become a missing person.

"Ok," she said, finally letting her guard down, realizing it might be in her best interest to try and trust this detective. But she needed to be careful not to share too much information. "The gang that seems to run the show at this casino—the Desperados, I think? —has been harassing my family."

"How so?"

"My husband filed a police report yesterday, so you should have all the information you need."

"What was the report for? What happened?" Detective Vasquez looked upset by this information.

What is this guy's deal?

"A rock was thrown through our window last night," she said. "We're not sure who did it, but I think it has something to do with this group. I think my husband is in trouble with them."

"I don't remember hearing a report like that," he replied. "But I will check with the station and see what I can find out. If you think this gang is after you, we need to ensure your house is safe. Do you understand?"

"No offense, but I'm not sure I totally trust the police to handle this," she said boldly, channeling her inner Hayden. "I'm scared of the potential fallout of you getting involved."

"Don't worry," he said, closing the gap between them and putting a hand on her shoulder. "I'm very discreet. I know how these guys work, and I know I can help you without anyone knowing you cooperated with me."

Cooperated. She shuddered. Maybe it was the wrong choice to give this detective any information. She didn't respond.

"Look," he said. "Why don't I come by your house tomorrow as a 'surprise visit,' and I can poke around and see if there's any evidence left behind."

"I don't know."

"I'm building a case against this gang, and any evidence we can find at your house could really help us. It's going to be big—a full boss takedown."

She thought about this. Maybe it would be a good thing to help get rid of the Desperados. It would benefit Hayden and his club, and maybe it could help save her from the danger she and Craig were in. Maybe she didn't need to be this damsel in distress any longer, relying on men to save her. Maybe she needed to take action to protect her own life.

"Ok," she said, giving in. She reluctantly gave him her cell phone number so they could schedule a time for him to come over.

"Don't worry," he said, reassuring her. "You're going to be safe now. I promise."

With that, he slipped quietly out of the restroom and left her standing there. She placed her hands on the edge of the sink and let out the deep breath she'd been holding, hoping she'd made the right choice.

She waited another moment to ensure Detective Vasquez would be far enough away from the entrance to eliminate suspicion before exiting the restroom. She reemerged through the hallway back into the neon casino, and looked for Hayden, but he was no longer sitting at the table where she'd left him. Scanning the room, she couldn't spot him, and her nerves resurfaced. *Hayden, where are you?*

As she stepped farther into the gambling den, she was startled by a fight breaking out at one of the nearby tables.

"You goddamned cheat!" she heard a man scream. "I'll fucking cut you!"

She locked eyes on the man who'd been screaming. She saw him spit into another man's face before punching him hard in the nose and shoving him onto the poker table, knocking chips and cards to the floor. More punches were exchanged. Drinking glasses broke, chairs were knocked over, and the room exploded into chaos. More men jumped into the fight as it evolved into a violent brawl.

The fighting was interrupted by three Hispanic men in cuts breaking through to the center and commanding the men to stop fighting. All three men had guns in their hands, pointed at the ground. *Shit.* Blake's heart was racing. The fighting immediately stopped, and the entire room fell silent, all eyes on this group.

"This motherfucker was counting cards!" the man yelled to the bikers.

One of the bikers turned to the accused man. "Is this true?"

"Of course not! I wouldn't even know how—" the accused man responded, but the dealer from their table chimed in.

"Either he was cheating or he's the luckiest *puta* to walk through these doors in a long time," the dealer said.

"Take him," the biker said to his fellow club members, waving his gun and pointing it to the dark hallway behind him. They grabbed the accused man by the arms and dragged him toward the back of the room, into the hallway, and through a pair of unmarked doors. The biker turned back to the table. Once his back was to her, she could make out the words on his cut. DESPERADOS MC. Underneath in smaller letters, CALIFORNIA. There was an image of two crossed pistols surrounded by flames.

Fire.

Is that Hector?

He gestured with his hand, and two large men appeared from the shadows.

"Remove this gentleman from our premises," he said, pointing his gun at the man who'd initiated the fight. "And if he tries to come back, don't be afraid to shoot him for trespassing."

The man tried to protest, but the men in the shadows surrounded him, pushing him toward the exit.

"I won't have fighting in my casino, *ese*," the biker said, finally putting his gun away in his pants pocket. "This is a place of business."

He turned away from the scene as the other two bikers dragged the man out of the casino.

Suddenly, hands were on her shoulders. She jumped.

"Seen enough?" Hayden whispered into her ear.

"Why are you always sneaking up behind me?"

"I'm not sneaking. You should be more aware of your surroundings."

She turned to face him. "Can we leave now?"

He nodded. "Let's go." Taking her hand again, he led her back through the crowd of tables and people, who'd returned their focus to their games now that the show was over. They stayed silent through the journey back out of the casino.

Once they exited the warehouse and returned to the safety of the fading afternoon light, she exhaled in relief that she did in fact escape the casino alive. She turned to Hayden.

"Was that Hector in there?"

"No," he said. "Hector rarely makes daytime appearances in that place."

"Oh." She was disappointed for some reason. "What do you think's gonna happen with that guy they took to that back room? The one accused of cheating."

"You sure you want to know?" he asked, raising an eyebrow.

"Yes."

"Desperados are known for their old school tactics."

"Meaning?"

"He'll probably lose a hand."

"Like...literally?" She was horrified.

He shrugged. "Or at least a finger or two."

"How will they know if he was actually cheating though?" she asked.

"Oh, that doesn't really matter. The fact that he was winning too much is probably enough for them."

She couldn't tell Hayden about Detective Vasquez. She needed him to trust her, and she knew that if she divulged the bathroom encounter, he'd somehow see it as her violating his trust or betraying him. *Better to keep it to myself.*

The setting sun chilled the air. She crossed her arms for warmth over her barely-there sundress as they headed back to her car.

"I overheard some interesting information while you were in the bathroom," he said, walking to the passenger side door of her car and opening it for her.

"Oh yeah?" she asked, sliding into her own passenger seat. He shut her in and walked around to the driver's side.

"Hand me my cut?" He motioned to the backseat as he settled in. She reached back and handed it to him. Rather than taking the hoodie off, he slid the cut over it and turned on the car.

"What did you hear?" she was afraid.

"I got close enough to a conversation to hear them talk about your husband. You sure you can handle hearing this?"

"Tell me."

"They were planning to kill him for not paying his debts. But they've given him another chance because they know about his job. They see dollar sign potential if they just wait it out."

"They said all of that out loud in that public place?" She was amazed.

"Of course not," he replied condescendingly. "I listened through one of the closed doors. They mostly used code, but I got the gist. *Fancy gringo executive.*"

"Oh. So, that's good news, right?" she asked.

He shook his head. "He would have had to offer up something big as collateral. They would never just take a chance like that, even with the promise of a future payout."

She thought about this. What could he have possibly given up as collateral? As far as she knew, all their assets were still in their possession. Unless there was another asset she didn't know about. At this point, it wouldn't surprise her to learn he had a secret house or boat or something. She was feeling more and more like she didn't know Craig at all. He was a stranger to her, filled with dark secrets.

"I can't think of anything right now that he would have traded, but I guess I don't really know anything about him."

Hayden placed his hand on her bare knee, rubbing it gently. He didn't say anything the rest of the drive. When they pulled up to Cold Spring Tavern, most of the motorcycles were gone, likely moved onto their next venue. Hayden parked her car next to his bike, shut the engine off, and climbed out.

She joined him outside, in between her car and his bike, waiting for him to make a move.

"I gotta run," he said. "Get home safe." He handed her the keys and leaned down to kiss her. Though it was now dark outside, they were still in plain view to any passersby, and this made her nervous...and excited. She kissed him back passionately, soaking in the taste of his mouth and the smell of his skin. As they pressed up against each other, she could tell he was hard again. *What is he, 18?*

"Ok, get out of here before I take you back into that bathroom," he growled at her, pushing her body away from his.

He hopped on his bike and sped off in the opposite direction of their houses. During her drive home, she replayed the day's events in her mind and worked on her story for Craig to explain why she'd been gone so many hours. As she pulled into her neighborhood, her phone vibrated aggressively in the center console. She glanced down and saw an unknown local number. Curious, she accepted the call through her Bluetooth.

"Hello?"

"Is this Blake?" a man's voice asked. Before she could answer, he followed up with, "This is Detective Vasquez."

"Oh," she said, startled. "Hi."

"Are you alone?"

"Yes, I'm just driving."

"Listen," he said. "I just checked the police reports from the past few days, and I didn't see anything for your address. I even checked with the state police just in case your husband filed through a different channel. Are you sure he actually filed the report?"

She was silent. "No," she finally answered.

"Do you have reason to believe he would lie to you about that?" he asked. When she was silent, he followed with, "How well do you know your husband?"

She didn't respond.

"I think you're in danger, Blake."

"What should I do?" she asked quietly.

"If your husband is caught up with these guys, the Desperados, then things could end really badly. If he lied about filing a report, my guess is either he's too afraid of what might happen, he's guilty of something, or both."

It's probably both. She was silent.

"Will you let me help you, Blake?" he pleaded desperately. "I don't want to see another pretty, innocent girl go missing."

Too bad I'm not innocent.

"What do we need to do?" she finally asked.

"I have an idea. I'll help keep you safe, and you'll help us take these guys down."

After they hung up, she felt nauseous. This was no longer just a one-sided conversation forced upon her in the women's restroom at the casino, where she could play the victim card if Hayden found out. She was now *cooperating* with the detective and was terrified Hayden would find out and think she'd betrayed him. But she also didn't want to die, and now that she'd seen more, learned more about the men who owned her husband, she felt more and more like that was going to be the inevitable outcome, even with Hayden protecting her.

By the time she pulled into her driveway, the sky was dark, and all the lights were on inside her house. She wondered if Craig had left at all that day. She remembered the bags of items from the hardware store in the trunk of her car and grabbed them before heading inside.

"Blake, that you?" Craig called from the garage.

"Hi," she responded, setting the bags down on the kitchen table. She walked into the garage. Craig had set up a woodworking station and was sawing down a slab of plywood. He'd taken off his sling and seemed to be using both arms decently now, but his bruises had reached that jaundiced stage of the healing process. He looked sick. "I grabbed the things you wanted at the store."

"Thanks, babe," he yelled over his power saw before turning it off, wiping sweat from his brow and standing up to face her. "You were gone a long time."

"I took myself shopping and out to dinner," she said quickly. "I needed a little time to decompress after what happened last night."

"All good, honey," he said, eyeing her barely-there dress and heels suspiciously. "But I was starting to get worried."

"Are you building a new window?"

"Just a temporary one made of wood until the guy can come next week," he said. "You came home at the perfect time actually. Where's the stuff you got from the store?"

"On the kitchen table," she said, automatically moving backward as he walked toward her. She was afraid she smelled like Hayden. Like sex. Like an underground casino. She didn't want Craig to get too close. "I'm going to hop in the shower. It's been a long day."

"Don't I get a kiss first?" he asked.

She felt her organs plummeting inside of her. *I don't want you to fucking touch me, you psycho. And I don't want you to taste another man on my lips.* But she saw no way out of this without raising suspicion.

"Of course," she finally said, bracing herself.

Craig moved toward her and placed his hand on her cheek, leaning his yellowing face in to kiss her gently on the lips. She was writhing internally. He didn't seem to notice anything was off.

"I'm sorry that this happened, and that you're afraid," he said, stroking her cheek, and tucking her hair behind her ear, his trademark move. "I promise I will handle this and make sure our home is safe, ok?"

Seems like everyone is promising me that lately.

"I'm not afraid," she lied. "Just needed to take a little time today."

"Enjoy your shower, babe."

My shower to wash off my indiscretions. Weird how the tables have turned.

When she returned to the living room in pajamas, her wet hair in a towel, she saw Craig was watching the news again. She followed his gaze to the TV and was horrified to see the latest breaking news.

A body had been found in the harbor.

Her legs turned to jelly, and she quietly fell into a chair beside Craig, eyes fixated on the TV.

"Police have quarantined the area as an active crime scene, and have shared little information with the public," the reporter was saying. "So far, the report notes that the body washed up on shore early this evening and appears to be an adult, but special circumstances will require more work to identify further details about the victim. This is being treated as a potential homicide and is an active investigation. Anyone with information is urged to reach out to our hotline listed at the bottom of the screen."

Blake's head was pounding. Was it Kendra's body? Did this "innocent" girl end up murdered? Was that going to be her fate too? And what did Craig know about this?

She looked over at Craig's face. His eyes were locked on the TV screen, his face stoic and hard to read.

"That's so awful," she said to him. He jumped in his seat, clearly unaware she'd even entered the room. And was he... sweating?

"I didn't see you there," he said, returning to his calm state.

"Do you think it's that missing girl?" she asked boldly, testing his reaction. "What was her name...Kendra?"

Craig's eye twitched when she said Kendra's name, and for a moment, she saw a glint of something in the twitchy eye. Was it guilt? Shame? *Malice*?

"Who knows," he said casually. "Sounds like the body is hard to identify."

Hard to identify. He sounded disassociated, removed from humanity, like a sociopath. *Is that what you are?*

They went to bed in silence that night. She didn't check to see if any lights were on in Hayden's house before joining her potentially dangerous husband in their shared bed. She was afraid but had become used to living in danger. It was like her brain and body now expected to always be in fight or flight mode, ready to take action at any moment. And miraculously, she slept hard that night despite the adrenaline pumping through her system.

The next morning, Craig was gone before she awoke. She'd slept through his alarm and him getting ready for work. Willing herself out of bed, she shuffled to the kitchen to brew coffee and wrap her brain around what her life had become, and what she would need to do to protect it. As she sipped on her first cup, she casually opened the kitchen curtains, telling herself it was to let the sunshine in, but really it was to see if anything was going on at Hayden's house. Things were seemingly quiet.

As if on command, her phone buzzed on the kitchen counter where it was charging. She picked it up. A text from Hayden. Swiping up, she opened the text.

> *H Money: Hey gorgeous. The crew and I are gonna be gone for a few days. Tail is still in place. Got a guy on standby if you need anything. Stay safe.*

Hayden's leaving. Panic surged inside of her. Though she didn't see him every day, knowing he and his friends were next door gave her a sense of safety amid the looming danger. Hayden being gone for a few days felt like her security blanket had been ripped off her, revealing, much to her surprise, staggering fear. *Guess I am a damsel.*

She set the phone down and took another sip of coffee while formulating a response. She didn't want to seem desperate or clingy. Finally, with a sigh, she picked her phone back up and typed an inauthentically cute response:

> *Blake: Ride safe, sexy {kissing emoji}*

She waited a few minutes to see if Hayden would respond, and when he didn't, a new idea surfaced in her mind. She impulsively dialed the last number that had called her the day before and listened to it ring.

"Detective Vasquez."

"Hi," she said, heart racing. "It's Blake. Can we talk?"

Chapter 14

Detective Vasquez arrived at her house promptly at 10 a.m., as they'd planned over the phone. She'd checked the perimeter of Hayden's house to ensure none of his club friends were home, and she knew there was no way Craig would leave the office before that evening. At her request, Vasquez parked his car a block away, and walked to her house dressed in street clothes. She didn't want to take any chances.

When he knocked on the door, she again peered out all the windows to confirm they were alone. All seemed quiet and empty. She shut the curtains. Opening the door, she urgently ushered him inside.

"Wow, you're really freaked, aren't you?" he said empathetically after she slammed the door shut behind him. He was carrying a large, ominous duffle bag.

"Just don't want to risk anyone seeing."

"Worried about your neighbors?" he asked, cocking an eyebrow, and nodding toward Hayden's house. "You really shouldn't be hanging out with those people. They're even worse than the Desperados." He shook his head in disgust. "They're next on my list, but we just don't have as good of a case built to take them down yet."

She shuddered. *Take down Hayden.* She could *not* let that

happen. She needed to keep the detective focused on the group that was terrorizing her, not on her new friends.

"Can I get you some coffee?" she asked, avoiding the topic.

"Coffee would be great," he said, setting his bag on her kitchen table. She eyed it nervously as she retrieved the coffee from her kitchen. She returned to the table with an already-brewed pot and two mugs.

"Cream or sugar?"

"Black is fine, thank you."

She poured coffee into both mugs, waiting for him to say something.

"Sorry about the neighbor comment. I'm not here to lecture you," he said, unzipping his bag on the table. "I'm here to help you."

He pulled out several electronic devices and sensors.

"Um, what is all of this?" *Stay calm.*

"State-of-the-art home security at its finest," he answered proudly, untangling wires and connecting different gadgets together. "I'm going to set up alarms on all doors and windows to monitor for any potential intruders. I'll also do a perimeter sweep to see if I can find any clues left behind by whichever Desperado threw the rock into your window."

"Why are you doing this for me?" she asked, suddenly suspicious. "You don't even know me."

"I'm protecting you from the bad guys," he said defensively. "And you're going to help me bring them down."

Red flag. Something felt off.

"Is this a typical service the police department offers its citizens?"

"Um, well..." he started, nervous. "I mean...no. It's not."

"I didn't think so." Her heart was racing. She calculated how long it would take to reach her phone if something went wrong. "What are you really doing here?"

He opened his mouth as if about to say something, but pursed his lips, not sure how to respond.

"Does anyone from your department even know you're here?" She could barely catch her breath now but didn't know how she could escape this situation.

"No," he admitted. "But I promise you there's no need to be afraid. It's not what you think. I really am here to help you."

"How do I know that?"

"Because...you look just like her."

"Who?"

"My girlfriend. Sarah," he said, tears filling his dark-circled eyes. "She was murdered last summer...by the Desperados."

Blake was dumbfounded. This was so unprofessional. And yet she felt herself letting her guard down. Maybe she'd had it wrong. He wasn't there at her house as a cop. He was there as a man seeking justice.

He blinked back tears and pointed to the kitchen table. "Can we talk?"

Blake nodded, and they sat down across from each other at the table.

"I'm sorry for coming on so strong," he apologized, choosing a mug, and taking a sip of the black coffee. "It's just that ever since her murder, I've been so laser focused on taking this gang down. They're good at covering their tracks, so it's been challenging securing enough evidence."

"And you think I can help you?" she asked skeptically, lifting her own mug to sip, trying to steady her hand from shaking.

"I think you're my best shot at getting to them."

"Why is that?"

"Two other women have gone missing since Sarah. They both had ties to these gangs." He paused and then added, "And I'm afraid you might be next."

Blake was silent, not sure how to respond.

"Anyway," he continued. "I'm sorry I scared you. But I just don't want to see another innocent go missing. I don't want what happened to Sarah or to any of the others to happen again."

"I get it," she said, feeling bad for this broken man. "Thank you for wanting to help."

"Is it ok if I set up this security system for you? I'd just feel a lot better knowing you're safe." Before she could respond, he added with more self-awareness, "Sorry if that's weird."

She nodded. He set his coffee mug down and stood up from the table. Grabbing a handful of devices, he walked toward the front door and began hooking up sensors around the entrance and windows. Once he was finished with the front, he worked his way around the perimeter of the house, finally disappearing into one of her bedrooms.

"These are all going to be really discreet, right?" she called through the wall as she poured herself another cup of coffee.

"No one will know unless they trip the alarm," he assured her. "Just make sure you and Craig are the only ones who have the code."

She scrolled through her phone to keep herself occupied as Vasquez secured her house. But she grew more anxious with every minute. Finally, she stood and wandered to the front entryway while he rigged her kitchen and backdoor, to inspect the new devices. At first, it didn't look like anything was there. She had to really search before spotting the microscopic sensor wedged into the window frame. *Almost undetectable.*

"Wow, these are so good," she said, turning around to face him. But he wasn't there. The door to the garage was open, so she walked to the doorway.

"All set," he said, walking toward her from the garage door. "Don't want to forget one of the most overlooked points of entry in a robbery: the garage door."

"I hadn't even thought of that," she said, feeling anxious. "Thank you."

"My pleasure," he said. "Mind if I finish my coffee?"

"Please," she said, gesturing to his seat.

As Vasquez sat back down at the table, she studied him. He was handsome in a sort of haunting way. While his skin was a deep tan color that radiated a healthy glow, he looked somewhat sickly. The way his luscious eyelashes surrounded his dark, sunken eyes, and set off his bony, angular jawline, there was a certain *heroin chic* vibe to him.

"I know I pushed this whole thing on you. I hope you don't feel like I'm overstepping."

She sipped her coffee. "Can I ask you something?"

"Sure," he said.

"That missing girl, Kendra," she said, cautiously reading his response. "Do you have any idea what happened to her?"

"I'm sorry, I can't divulge details of an open case with you, other than what's available publicly."

"But the body they found last night," she said, bolder. "In the harbor."

"I...really can't say anything," he repeated.

"I think we're past professionalism at this point. Don't you?" She gestured to the well-hidden alarms.

He sighed. "The body wasn't hers."

"How do you know?"

"Because the body they found was a male."

Not Kendra.

"Why didn't they share that on the news?" she asked, wondering how much she could get out of him.

"Because it's a sensitive case. It would be hard to reveal the gender of the victim without revealing more...gruesome details."

"Look. I'm not some nosy bystander. This affects me. I'm scared." She played up the damsel thing. "You keep telling me about girls going missing who are mixed up with this gang. And here's one that's plastered all over the news."

"What do you know about Kendra?" Vasquez was suddenly suspicious.

"What do you mean?" she asked stupidly, looking into her coffee mug.

"You said she was 'mixed up with this gang.' What do you know about that?"

Blake was silent.

"There's more you're not telling me, isn't there?"

"Do you want something stronger than coffee?" she asked.

As Blake poured Detective Vasquez a second tequila (she'd grabbed a bottle from Craig's high-end collection), she noticed him briefly check out her body in her peripheral vision. *Maybe flirting is a better way to get information. He did, after all, buy a home security system for my house with his own money to try and protect me.*

"So, you really don't know this Kendra, then?" he asked, sitting back in his chair and sipping the tequila.

"No," she lied. "I just overheard someone at a bar the other day talking about her."

His facial expression indicated disbelief. She needed to lie

163

better.

"Her picture was being shown on one of the TVs at the bar," she continued. "I heard some guys pointing at the screen and saying something about...'serves her right for getting mixed up with Desperados.'"

She took a sip of her own tequila, hoping she'd convinced him.

Vasquez was silent for a moment, studying her. Then a smile creeped onto his face. "You're good at getting information from people, aren't you?"

She smiled deviously.

"I don't know if it's your persuasion skills or the tequila," he mused. "But I think maybe you missed your calling as a cop."

"I don't think I could pull off the uniform," she joked.

"That's why I became a detective, so I don't have to wear one."

"I'll cheers to that," she flirted.

"How about we cheers to your bravery." He held out his glass toward her.

"My bravery?"

"You could have shut down and gone into hiding from all this shit. Most people would. But you...you're taking action. You're taking control of the situation. That takes balls."

"Fair enough," she said, clinking her glass into his. "So, do you have any idea whose body it was that they found?" She'd gotten this far. Maybe a little flirting could get her all the answers.

"Now you're just taking advantage."

She didn't respond. She just smiled, waiting for him to continue.

"Alright, fine, if you think you can handle it."

"I can handle it."

"Well, it will be difficult to determine the identity of the victim," he paused dramatically, "because all of his fingers and teeth were removed before his body was burned to a crisp."

She was silent.

"Yeah," he said. "Pretty brutal."

They sipped their tequila in silence.

"Had to be the Army of Outlaws," he said, breaking the silence.

Her heart skipped a beat. "Why would you say that?"

"That's their M.O."

The man in the shed. It hit her with absolute certainty. The body was Robert's. *The man I helped kill.*

"But it's been years since we've been able to pin any murders on them," he continued. "Like the Desperados, they're good at covering their tracks."

"Maybe it wasn't them," she offered.

"Don't be naïve," he said, setting his empty glass down. He looked up at the clock—12:30 p.m. "I've taken up too much of your day."

He stood up from the table, and she followed the gesture, ready for him to leave. The longer he stayed at her house, the higher the odds were of someone finding out. After he packed up his belongings, he looked into her eyes.

"Blake, please try to do me a favor?"

"What's that?"

"Don't disappear."

Instant chills. "I'll do my best."

Blake paced around her house that evening, glass of pinot noir in hand, waiting for Craig to come home. She'd worked on her story all afternoon and was prepared. She showered, did her make-up, and put on her favorite black jumpsuit that hit her curves in all the right spots. Casual but sexy. She'd even cooked dinner to help ensure Craig would be in a good mood.

By the time she heard the front door unlock, she was tipsy, having moved onto wine after the tequila with Detective Vasquez. *Oops, I forgot to eat today.*

"Hey, babe," Craig said as he entered their home. "Smells good in here!"

"I made a stir fry with that sauce you like."

"That's sweet of you." He walked into the kitchen and kissed her on the lips. *I hate you I hate you.*

"You've had a tough couple of weeks, and I wanted to do something nice." The lie tasted bitter on her tongue as she poured them each a glass of wine. Not that she needed another.

As they sat down to eat, she took a deep breath and prepared to launch into her memorized speech.

"I have some good news," she said.

"Oh yeah?" He seemed intrigued as he took another bite of food.

"I had a security system installed today."

"What?" He looked panicked. "In the house?"

"No, in the forest." She tried to course correct her sarcasm to sound more like teasing. "Of course, in the house."

"Why would you do that?" He was agitated now, setting his fork down.

"Because we needed it. That rock coming through window the other night really scared me."

"I know, but you should let me take care of these things. I'm the man."

So now you're sexist too?

"You're busy with work, and I had the time."

"Where did you even find this security system? Is it legit?"

"Of course," she defended. "It's a local company. I saw an ad online for same-day installation."

"So, you just let strangers into the house?" He was fuming. "Blake, you're so naïve sometimes."

That was the second time she'd been called naïve that today. Now she was fuming too.

"How is that naïve? I did what you failed to do—make our home safe."

"What the hell are you talking about? I fixed the window. I called the police and filed a report."

Liar liar liar. "And what ever happened with that?" she challenged. "Why haven't they been back to check on us or follow up?"

"Because some kid throwing a rock through our window is probably the least of their concerns right now, *sweetie*," he patronized, standing up from the table. "Haven't you heard? There are missing girls and dead bodies and other bigger things happening in this town."

He had a point. He'd always been a decent storyteller, and now he was using that skill to continue his arrogant lies while making her sound stupid for questioning them.

"I can't believe you're angry with me for making our house secure." She guided the conversation back to the original point.

"I'm angry with you for doing something like that without talking to me first."

"Why, because you're *the man?*"

"No, because we're partners and should consult each other on these things," he said. Then with what looked like angry impulse, added, "And, honestly, I'm the only one contributing financially right now, and you're spending the money *I make* for us on stupid shit that we don't need."

Rage erupted inside her. "The money *you make*?" She laughed angrily, standing up from the table to face him. "I knew you'd throw that in my face! You're the one who told me to take a break from working when we moved here. I loved my job back in Phoenix, and you took that from me! It's your fault I'm not *contributing financially*."

"You're right," he said, to her surprise. "I'm sorry."

But she wasn't about to let him off the hook so easily, not after weeks of knowing all of his lies and having to pretend like everything was fine.

"Where is this mystery money you're talking about?" she challenged. "Because I haven't seen our bank account balances increase lately."

"What's that supposed to mean?"

"Are we in trouble financially?" She wanted to see how he'd handle the lie when confronted directly. "Are you gambling again?"

"Why would you ask that?" He was defensive. "You know I go to meetings twice a week."

"How do I know you're not off gambling somewhere instead?"

"Don't I keep this roof over our heads?" he demanded, avoiding the question. "Isn't there food in the kitchen, gas in our cars, clothes on our backs? I *know* you've made a few trips to Sephora lately. So, tell me, princess, what am I not giving you?"

The truth.

"I'm going out," she said, backing away from him. "The code for the security system is on the fridge under the Tahiti magnet from our honeymoon. Punch it in once to turn it on, and again to turn it off."

"You better not be driving," he said coldly. "I could smell your breath from five feet away when I got home."

"I'm fine!" she yelled, grabbing her purse and slamming the door shut behind her.

Climbing into her car, she realized she was in fact a little impaired and probably shouldn't be driving. But her need to make a dramatic exit outweighed her sense of self preservation. Since it was only 7:30 p.m., the coffee shop down the street would still be open, so she decided to go caffeinate.

Sipping her espresso in the coffee shop parking lot, she scrolled through Instagram on her phone. She stopped when she saw an ad for Harley Davidson. *Ha, that's some specific targeting.* With her brain still clouded and uninhibited from the wine, she sent Hayden a text.

Blake: Any chance you're still in town?

A text bubble popped up, like he was typing. Then the typing stopped. Nothing. She waited. Still nothing. He was leaving her on read. She went back to Instagram to try and distract herself while she waited for him to text back. Her phone finally vibrated.

Craig: Please come home. Let's talk.

She replied instantly.

Blake: I need to cool off. I'll be home later. Don't wait up.

She angrily went back to scrolling. Finally, after another 10 minutes of her coming out of her buzzed haze, her phone vibrated again.

H Money: In Oxnard. What's up?

Blake: I need an escape.

H Money: Come escape at the club house.

Blake: I thought your house was the club house?

H Money: Nah baby girl. That's the annex. Where the kids throw parties. Club house is in Oxnard.

She felt stupid. This whole time she'd thought her next-door neighbors' frat house was the official club house for their chapter. But it made sense to her now why only young guys seemed to live there. It was the party house.

Blake: You sure it's ok for me to come?

H Money: {Current location shared}

Guess so. She pasted the pin drop into her navigation app. Only a few miles. She felt mostly sober by this point anyway. Digging into her purse, she found breath mints and gum and was relieved to be able to freshen her breath. After touching up her make-up in the rearview mirror, leveraging the compact and lipstick she'd also found in her purse, she turned the car on and headed toward Oxnard. Toward Hayden.

Chapter 15

As she neared Hayden's pin-dropped location, she took a wrong turn and drove first through the charming part of downtown Oxnard Shores. It was inviting with a similar aesthetic to Ventura, and she wondered why she'd never thought to explore the area before. But as she course-corrected, she was navigated inland toward the hills which had always been rumored to house resident gangs. *And apparently motorcycle clubs too.*

She drove down the streets of Oxnard and noticed the subtle differences in how people dressed in this city. Unlike the sporty paddleboarders of Santa Barbara and the skaters of Ventura, the male inhabitants walking the nighttime streets of Oxnard donned long, baggy jean shorts paired with shin-high white socks and skater shoes. Some wore wide-rimmed baseball hats with the rim flipped up, while others expressed themselves with long goatees and other tough-looking but clearly high maintenance facial hair. There was constant 805 signage, to represent the local area code and a sense of Central Coast pride. And unlike the yoga moms of Santa Barbara and the Free People hippies of Ventura, the women of Oxnard wore retro, low-rise jeans and crop tops, proud to show off their bodies no matter how thin or thick.

Her navigation prompted her to turn into a seedier neighborhood lined with dive bars and pawn shops. Behind the third pawn shop at the end of one block, she finally spotted it. The club house.

In a rather large piece of corner real estate, she saw a black-painted building with the Army of Outlaws MC logo broadcast proudly on the front. On the left-hand side was a concrete walled walkway with steps to the front door beneath the intimidating signage, and on the right-hand side around the corner, facing the other street, was a large garage which was currently closed by one of those industrial, metal doors.

Why didn't I ever bother to Google their headquarters before? Her heart was racing, per usual. Once parked, she shut off her engine and grabbed her denim jacket from the backseat, sliding it over her black maxi dress. She pulled her phone from the center console and swiped open to text Hayden.

Blake: I'm out front

No response. She waited another minute, anger and rejection quickly surfacing inside her. *He better fucking answer after I just drove all the way out here.*

Just as her rage peaked, she jumped dramatically at a knock on her driver's side window. Hayden was standing outside, looking concerned by her overreaction.

She unlocked and opened her door, sliding out of the car with as much grace and composure as possible.

"Didn't mean to scare you," he teased. He looked delicious as ever in his leather jacket, crisp, white V-neck shirt, and jeans. He had another gaudy belt buckle on, which weirdly turned her on. His facial hair was starting to grow longer than his normal scruff into a fuller beard, and his long, dark, wavy hair was pulled back into a bun.

"I'm not scared," she lied, for the fiftieth time since she'd moved to the Central Coast.

"Good." He smiled, showing off his dimples. "Because you're about to enter the lion's den."

"Good thing I brought my whip."

He raised an eyebrow and grabbed her hard by the waist, pulling her into an embrace. "Love your spontaneity tonight," he whispered into her ear, before dragging her toward the concrete wall leading up to the club house.

"Just be cool," he warned. And while she had the urge to retort with something sarcastic in response, she recognized the seriousness in his tone and decided not to respond. Instead, she let him lead her by the hand into the interior of the black-painted, unapproachable building.

Upon entering, she was surprised to see what looked like a regular bar. A regular bar with another giant Army of Outlaws logo on the wall, and more insignia plastered all over the room. There was a bartender serving drinks to men and women perched on barstools, people playing pool under the dim lighting, and groups huddled inside tacky, red, vinyl booths. But all the men were wearing Army of Outlaws cuts, and many of the women had matching paraphernalia—women's tank tops and jackets with Army of Outlaws MC logos and slogans. *Like gang swag.* Her public relations background propelled the thought. *Maybe the girls picked those up at a biker convention. Or maybe they're like Mardi Gras beads, where they get them for showing their tits.* She smirked a little.

But as Hayden led her through the room, which was basically one, large advertisement for their club, all eyes turned to her. Everyone had judgment in their eyes. Disturbed by her presence. Angry. Their stares quickly wiped the smile off her face.

Finally, as he led her to an empty space at the bar, she recognized some familiar faces. The cocaine girls from the wake.

"Blake Lively!" the rail-thin, tiny one called to her, hopping off her stool and approaching her, beer in hand. She was wearing a tiny, black wife beater with the slogan, "The Wild Never Die," in white, and the Army of Outlaws logo in smaller print beneath it. Her entire bare midriff was exposed, and her low-rise jeans were belted with one of those black, leather spiked belts from the old days of *Hot Topic*.

"Nikki, hey," Blake responded with a smile, praying she'd gotten the name right.

"Didn't expect to see you here," she said snidely, sniffling. She looked at Hayden suspiciously, but continued speaking to Blake. "This doesn't seem like your kind of place."

"I'm always up for trying new things." Blake tried to sound friendly.

"Nikki, get over here!" Brittany, the friend with the huge boobs pushed up to her neck by a corset, called from farther down at the bar. "Jesse and Big Dog are taking us shooting."

"About goddamn time!" Nikki yelled back, turning away from Blake without a goodbye.

"Yo, Prospect," a supersized, at least 6'5, man standing next to Brittany—*I'm guessing that's Big Dog*—called over to one of the red, vinyl tables of drinkers. "Go grab our artillery. Don't forget the Winchester and Remington. We *hunting* tonight!"

A short, stocky man urgently stood up from his table, obeying Big Dog, and walked briskly toward the double doors in the back. He was wearing a cut, but it didn't have the same patches on it as the other men. Fumbling with a key, he opened one of the doors and disappeared behind it. Blake wasn't quick enough to glimpse what was behind the doors before it slammed shut.

When she turned back to face Hayden, she realized he'd moved to the bar and was ordering drinks. "Tito's soda for the lady, and a Four Roses for me, neat," he said to the bartender, a burly guy also in a cut. *Thank god I sobered up before I came.* As the burly bartender turned his back on them to mix the drinks, Blake noticed his cut was also missing some patches, like the prospect retrieving the guns for Big Dog. He sheepishly handed them their drinks, looking nervous.

"Come on," Hayden teased the bartender. "Where's that famous smile that's supposed to come with my service?"

The bartender smiled uneasily. "Sorry, man."

"That's more like it," Hayden said, taking his drink, handing Blake hers, and then nudging her away from the bar. "Good prospect."

I guess club members don't pay around here.

Hayden whispered, "Follow me," in her ear, guiding her toward the back of the room where the prospect had disappeared to gather the guns. As she followed him, she felt angry eyes penetrating her with every step. Distrust of the outsider.

Hayden opened the now unlocked back door and pushed her inside. She stepped through the threshold, nervous to find out what was on the other side, and as she entered a new hallway, realized she was in what looked more or less like an office building. There were several closed doors lining the hallway to the left, and a larger room to the right with a plaque next to the door that said COUNCIL.

"What's in there?" she asked.

"Where all the magic happens, baby," he said haughtily. He

grabbed her butt cheek hard as she turned from him. "You look hot in this dress, by the way."

"I've never met anyone who compliments my outfits as much as you," she said, playfully brushing him off.

"Mama raised me right," he replied. "I've also never met anyone who manages to always look as fuckable as you."

Before she could respond, he opened the door to the room with the COUNCIL plaque. "Because I like that ass so much, I'll give you a little peek."

They entered the room. Inside was a large, wooden table with uneven edges and imperfections in the surface. Flowing down the center of the table was what looked like a brilliant blue river current crafted from an epoxy resin. It was a remarkable piece of furniture, something she wouldn't have expected to exist in this place. The table was surrounded by beautifully ornate wooden chairs, each one slightly different than the next. Definitely handmade. On the walls were rows of framed photos, showcasing members of the club from each year. She smiled.

"What are you smiling about?"

"It's cute." She laughed.

"*Cute?*" He smiled back evilly, his blue eyes piercing her. "What about this is *cute* to you?"

"All these group photos. It's like your own version of a yearbook." She laughed, hoping to lighten the mood.

But he seemed to take offense to her laughter. He was no longer smiling. He rushed toward her, pulling her waist hard into him with one hand, and grabbing her by the throat with his other tattooed hand. He pressed gently, threatening. She could still breathe but understood the message he was sending: her life was literally in his hand. She didn't resist. She didn't want him to think she was a coward. *He won't hurt me.*

"Let me tell you about those pictures," he said gently into her ear, still not letting go of her throat. He pushed harder, limiting her air supply. "Look closely at the members from year to year."

He finally released his hand and she inhaled audibly. He stroked her cheek, then turned her head toward the row of photos. She was silent, waiting.

"The only way out of this club is by death, sickness, or exile. You see how some members have changed in the photos over the years?" He gently pointed her head toward the second-to-last photo, the previous year. "Just know there are only three possible reasons why a few from last year are missing from this year's photo."

For the first time standing in Hayden's presence, she was afraid. All this time, she thought she'd figured out who the bad guys were, who to trust and where to align her loyalty. Yes, Hayden and his friends had locked up a man in their shed, murdered him and dismembered his body, but the man they'd killed had raped and murdered *their* friend first. It was retaliation, not cold-blooded murder. She'd almost likened them to local superheroes. But now her fantasy was shattering, and she understood that the Army of Outlaws was just as dangerous as the Desperados. Hayden had essentially implied they were capable of murdering their own. And he'd just shown a darker side of himself that she'd never seen before. She'd thought, as an innocent, she could be an exception to his outlaw lifestyle, but realized now that there was more to him than just the bad-boy-biker facade. There was an underlying propensity toward violence.

"I didn't mean to offend you," she finally said, rubbing her throat where he'd held it.

His guard immediately dropped at this helpless gesture, and he pulled her into his arms, holding her protectively, back to his usual self. "I'm sorry. Did I hurt you?" He tilted her chin up to face him.

"No, it's fine," she said, still rattled.

The door swung open forcefully, interrupting them. Rocco stood in the doorway. When he saw Blake in the room, he looked enraged.

"*The president* wanted me to come tell you there's a meeting here in five minutes. You all need to be here for it."

"Thanks, bro," Hayden said. When Rocco lingered in the doorway, Hayden followed up with, "Anything else?"

"She shouldn't be in here," Rocco said, gesturing to Blake while addressing only Hayden.

"Relax, I'm taking her to my room in a second."

Rocco looked irritated, but left the room, closing the door behind him.

"Let's go," he said, ushering her toward the door.

"You have a room here?" she asked quietly, following him out of the meeting room and down the other side of the hallway toward the rows of closed doors.

"I sometimes crash here."

He stopped in front of a door with the number 3 on it and pulled out keys from his pocket to unlock and open. Another Hayden room with another locked door. *I wonder how many women he's brought here, when it's more convenient than his other bedroom in Ventura.*

As they entered the room, she was surprised to see a very spartan setting: a perfectly made futon bed, a small dresser, desk, and a bar cart. The wall above the futon bed had a single push-pinned Army of Outlaws MC poster. The same "The Wild

Never Die" saying from Nikki's wife beater was on display in large font above the room's only window. There was a rustic-looking sign that said "1%" on it above the bar cart. She recognized 1% from a patch Hayden wore on his cut and made a mental note to Google that later.

"Nice room."

"It's not much, but it's a good crash pad," he said, smiling his magnetic smile at her. "I gotta go to this meeting real quick. Are you cool chilling in here?"

"No problem," she said, assessing she didn't really have a choice.

"Help yourself to my liquor." He winked at her as he left the room.

She walked over to the bar cart and examined the options. Whiskey, whiskey, more whiskey, gin, tequila. *Tequila it is.* The tequila triggered her memory from that morning. *Please, please, please don't let anyone have seen Detective Vasquez at my house.*

As she sipped her tequila, she felt on edge, trapped in this new prison cell. Her curiosity about Hayden's impromptu nighttime meeting was eating away at her, and she became aware of how late it was getting. She checked her phone. 9 p.m. Craig would start to worry. Not that she cared how he felt anymore, but she didn't want him blowing up her phone, or worse, calling the police. She talked herself into leaving this strange place, and set her glass down, preparing for her exit.

Poking her head out the door, she saw the hallway was empty and decided to make a run for it. But as she tiptoed down the hall, she heard voices coming from the COUNCIL room. Not able to resist the urge to listen, she froze and tilted her ear toward the closed door.

Though muffled, she picked up on a few soundbites:

"Red and Dave are en route to the pickup," she heard Hayden say.

"Those two dickheads better not fuck this up," another voice said. "This is the motherload. Since we opted for more kilos per order to have less frequent pickups, we need this first transfer to go smoothly."

So, they're drug dealers.

"They can handle this," Hayden said, defending his friends. "They know the consequences of this going south."

"Good," the other voice replied. "Send three more guys to tail them to the drop-off. We need to make sure they're not followed."

"Hey!" an angry voice shouted behind Blake. She turned to see Rocco glaring at her. "What the fuck do you think you're doing?"

"I...I was just looking for the bathroom," she lied.

"You shouldn't be back here," he grumbled. Then he sighed. "Follow me."

She did as she was told, following Rocco back down the dark hallway toward a door on the far-right side. He unlocked the door and opened it, gesturing for her to enter.

"Thanks." she smiled, trying to incite compassion in him with her politeness.

She walked into the bathroom, but as she turned around to lock the door behind her, Rocco pushed her hard by the chest, causing her to lose her balance and fall backward into the bathroom sink. She caught herself by gripping the countertop, and shakily stood up to face him. He silently stepped into the bathroom and closed the door behind him. Then he locked it.

"What is it about you privileged suburban girls?" he asked, edging toward her. "Why do you stick your nose where it doesn't belong?"

She didn't respond. She clutched the sink, frozen. Waiting.

"You don't come from this world," he continued, his face now just inches from hers. "You don't *belong* here."

"I'm just hanging out with Hayden," she finally said, attempting to deescalate the situation. "I'm not trying to stick my nose in anyone's business, I swear."

"Yeah. *Hayden.* That pretty boy should know better." He reached his hand out and entwined his dirty fingers in her blonde hair. "But now that I'm up close, I can see why he might forget who he is when he's around you. You're gorgeous. Like some high society siren, seducing us Outlaws, one by one."

"I don't want any trouble," she said quietly, panicking.

He grabbed her hair hard in his fist, yanking her head down to the side.

"I bet you like it rough too," he said, pressing his body into hers and forcing his mouth on hers, planting unreciprocated kisses while holding her tightly by the hair and pinning her against the sink with his legs. "Wanna show me why Hayden keeps you around? If you're a good girl for me, maybe I'll be nicer to you." He pushed her denim jacket off her shoulder with his free hand and tugged down the top of her jumpsuit, forcefully grabbing her breast and squeezing hard. She let out a cry.

"Please don't do this," she begged, but he kept pushing, kept forcing himself.

She turned inward to find strength. *Fight or flight. Fight or flight. Fight. I have to fight.* She used all the strength in her body to free one of her legs, and then kneed him in the balls as hard as she possibly could.

His grip on her hair immediately loosened, and he pulled

back, stunned, crying out in pain. She used this opportunity to sprint to the door, unlock it, and run before Rocco could stop her.

As she sprinted down the hallway, she saw that the council meeting room was now empty. *Fuck.* She ran toward the doors leading to the front area and pushed through them. Reemerging into the Army of Outlaws bar, she tried to calm her demeanor, so as not to alarm the other patrons or draw attention to herself. She adjusted her dress and jacket, straightening herself out and walking as casually as she could through the room. No Hayden in sight. She could feel the eyes of the other patrons on her. She had to get out of there. Keeping her eyes focused on the exit, she held her breath the entire length of the room. Despite all eyes burning into her, she refused to look up and make eye contact with any of them. She was afraid if she lost momentum, Rocco would catch up with her.

She let out her held breath as she exited the bar, welcoming the chilled air against her face, a signal that this nightmare was almost over.

"You're a real homie hopper, aren't you?" a woman's voice said from behind her.

She turned around and saw Christina lurking in the shadows, a lit cigarette in hand and an oversized, puffy coat cradled around her skimpy dress. She was leaning against the wall next to the now open garage attached to the building.

"Excuse me?"

Christina emerged from the shadows, taking a long puff of her cigarette from her overly lined rep lips. Her eyeliner was winged out dramatically, making her look catlike. She was trashy, but beautiful. "I mean, Hayden I get. He's gorgeous. But Rocco? A little bit of a downgrade if you ask me."

"What are you talking about?" Blake asked aggressively.

"You and Rocco going into the bathroom together," she said, smiling widely, her eyes evil.

"Look, I don't know what you thought you saw, but—"

"I saw a blonde wannabe-mama trying to suck as many Outlaw dicks as she can to get in with the club."

"I didn't *go* into that bathroom with Rocco," Blake argued. "He followed me in and—"

"Tried to force himself on you?" Christina interrupted, unsurprised by the notion.

"Yes."

"Yeah, sounds like him." She looked empathetic for a moment, but quickly shook off the brief humanity and took another hit of her cigarette. "That's not what I told Hayden though."

"Where is Hayden?" Blake asked.

"He and his friends just left on their bikes. Some urgent mission or something."

"What did you tell him about me?"

"I told him I saw you wait for him to go into his meeting, and then you snuck off with Rocco." She laughed. "And I *may* have said it wasn't the first time I'd seen you two sneaking around together."

"Why would you do that?" Blake asked stupidly.

"Because Hayden is mine," Christina replied. "Maybe he doesn't know it yet, but he and I are meant for each other. I'm gonna be his old lady someday. You're just a temporary plaything for him."

"Yeah, you sound really confident about that," Blake shot back sarcastically. "Maybe he'd want you more if you stopped trying so hard."

"Don't fuck with me, bitch," Christina threatened. She flicked her lit cigarette at Blake's feet. "I have powerful friends."

"Then go back inside and play with them," Blake patronized, turning her back on Christina, and walking quickly toward her car.

Once inside, she immediately locked the doors and gunned it out of there. As she reached the 101 freeway and increased her speed, her brain registered the freedom, and she broke down in violent sobs as she gripped the steering wheel.

Chapter 16

By the time Blake pulled into her driveway at 11 p.m., she'd collected herself and erased all signs she'd been crying. Craig opened the front door as she exited her car, meeting her out front. Clearly, he'd been waiting up for her and watching the driveway all night.

"I'm sorry, honey," he blurted out before she was even at the front steps. "I totally overreacted earlier."

She sighed. She didn't want to fight with him. She was exhausted. And she still needed to continue playing dumb until she could ensure they'd get their money and be rid of Hector. She'd already said too much to him when she questioned him about the money.

"Me too," she finally willed herself to say.

After setting the alarm on their new security system, they went to bed in silence that night, but she let Craig fall asleep with his arm around her before sliding away from him to the other side of the bed.

The next morning, after Craig left for work, Blake headed to the grocery store. She had an emotional hangover from the night before and really didn't feel like shopping, but their house was out of the essentials: coffee and wine.

As she perused the liquor aisle at their local mom-and-pop

store, she crouched down to study the Pinot Noir section, which always had good local options.

"Blake is that you?" a woman's voice said behind her.

Blake shot up to her feet from her crouching position. *Please don't be a biker chick.*

When she turned around, the woman standing there was not a biker chick. She had a simple, elegant, long bob, and was wearing pearls and a cardigan. Bill's wife.

"Sarah," Blake feigned her best affable voice. She'd successfully avoided having to endure any further social interactions with Playboy Bill and Simple Sarah since their dinner in Santa Barbara. "How are you?"

"Oh, you know," she said sadly, her usually aloof demeanor seeming more down to earth. "Could be better." Then she looked sympathetically at Blake. "But I can't even imagine what you must be going through."

What is this bitch talking about?

Registering that she was missing something, but not wanting to seem disconnected from her husband, Blake took a risk with her response. "I'm doing ok."

"I just feel so bad for Bill and Craig, you know?" Sarah seemed out of sorts, like she'd just finished crying. "I mean, *we'll* be ok. Bill is on the board of several other companies, and we have my family's money of course. But Craig. And you. You two *moved* here for this job. Bought a house. Are you sure you'll be ok?"

So, Craig lost his job. "We're scrappy," Blake said, doing her best to bury the shock she felt from appearing on her face. "We always land on our feet."

When Sarah lingered, gripping the handle of her shopping cart anxiously, clearly hoping for a longer exchange, Blake seized the opportunity to get more details.

"So, how much information did Bill tell you?" she asked, friendly. "Craig didn't tell me much. I think he's too upset."

"All I know is that the big acquisition deal fell through, and it had something to do with the company's financial reports that Bill and Craig put together. The CEO needed a fall guy...or *guys*, I suppose. So, they were both let go. That's all he told me."

"So crazy," Blake said, trying to sound like this wasn't brand-new information. "How's Bill doing?"

"He's been a mess for days," she said despondently. *Days.* "Haven't been able to get him to leave the house. That's why I'm here—I'm planning to cook his favorite meal tonight to try and lift his spirits."

Craig lost his job days ago. She didn't know how many days, but he'd been "going to work" every day that week. Where was he really going?

"That's sweet of you. I'm trying to lift Craig's spirits with actual spirits." Blake gestured to the wine, hollowly attempting a joke.

Sarah fake laughed, and then excused herself to leave. "I wish you all the best," she said formally, before rolling her shopping cart away.

Once home, Blake paced the house. *Where the hell is Craig? Was he planning to tell me he'd lost his job? Where is he going every day? Is he at the casino? Is he with Kendra? Does he know where Kendra is? What the hell is going on?* She popped the cork on one of the new local Pinots and sipped with intention. She looked out the kitchen window. No one appeared to be home at Hayden's. She hadn't heard from him since the night before when he'd ditched her at the club house, and at this point, she was pretty sure he thought she'd betrayed him by hooking up with another club member. What was it that Christina had called her? A "wannabe-mama"? *What even is that?* She wanted to correct the cruel misinformation but didn't feel like it would be effective through text. She needed to see Hayden in person. But Hayden was gone. He'd said he would be gone for days in his text the previous morning. She had no idea when he'd be home.

She spent the rest of the day cleaning the house and doing chores to keep her mind off the many things she couldn't control. After polishing off a bottle of wine while polishing the wood floors, she eventually ran out of busywork. So, she climbed into her coziest pajamas with sushi characters on them and turned on Netflix.

Around 9 p.m., Craig stumbled in the front door, clearly drunk. Blake shot up from the couch.

"Craig?" she asked cautiously, slowly moving toward him.

"Hey, babyyyyy," he slurred, kicking his shoes off, and proceeding to trip over them and tumble forward, landing hard on the freshly polished floor.

"Craig, are you ok?" She was alarmed by how inebriated he was. He never got that drunk. He'd drink, but he was never out of control. She helped him to his feet and guided him to the couch.

"Sit there," she ordered. "I'll get you some water."

"I'm so sorry," he whimpered.

"I know," she said, returning with the water.

"No, you don't," he insisted. "You don't know."

"What don't I know, Craig?"

"How sorry I am." He gulped the water down in one swig, slamming the empty glass on the coffee table.

"For being drunk?" she asked.

"For everything."

Was he about to confess?

"I've been a bad...bad..." He trailed off, his eyes closed. He looked borderline blacked-out.

"What have you done that's bad?" *Admit what you've done. Admit to it, you son of a bitch.*

"Literally everything." He let his head fall back against the couch, slouching down into it. He was falling asleep.

Clearly, she wasn't going to get anywhere with him. "Come on," she said, standing up and walking to the front door to set the alarm code before returning to hold out her hand. "Let's get you to bed."

Once she'd helped Craig into bed, she climbed in next to him, wide awake.

"Blake?" he asked. He sounded small, like a little boy. "I'm so sorry. For everything."

"I know," she said. She could never forgive him, even if he came clean eventually. But she pitied him. He sounded so sad. So pathetic.

It took Blake a long time to fall asleep that night due to Craig's drunken snores, but eventually she found herself drifting off.

"WAKE THE FUCK UP!"

Blake shot up in bed. Still half asleep, she wondered if she was inside a nightmare. But as she opened her eyes wide in the dark, she could make out something floating in front of her—a silvery, glimmering piece of metal. At that moment, she understood that it was no nightmare. There were shadowy figures standing all around the bed. People. In her bedroom. She felt Craig next to her, also upright.

189

One of the shadowy figures moved toward Craig's side of the bed, approaching the bedside table. The figure clicked on the lamp.

As her eyes adjusted, she witnessed the horror in front of her: three men in black ski masks pointing long, skinny guns at them.

"Wake up, *putas!*" one man yelled, laughing. The others joined in.

Two guns on Craig. One gun on her, pointed directly at her face.

This was the first time Blake had ever had a gun pointed at her. It felt like what she'd always imagined it would feel like: pure adrenaline and panic, like it could be lights out at any second. She felt every inch of her skin sweating and buzzing, and it took all of her self-control not to shake, or worse, cry.

"Please," Craig implored. "Please don't hurt us. We'll give you whatever you want!"

"That's adorable," the man with his gun pointed at Blake said to Craig. There was something clipped onto the gun that extended its length and made it look awkwardly long. *A silencer?*

"Get up! Both of you."

Blake immediately did as she was told and climbed out of bed. She stood there, waiting for further instruction. Craig fumbled as he slowly wobbled up from the bed, clearly still a little drunk. She had no idea how long they'd been asleep.

"Out into the living room," the man ordered, pointing his gun toward the hallway.

Blake and Craig walked slowly out of the bedroom and into the living room, with the three guns pointed on them.

"On your knees. And face the wall."

Blake and Craig got down onto their knees, side-by-side. The room fell silent. *What is happening?* The masked men behind her weren't making a sound, but she was too afraid to turn around and face them. Instead, she stayed frozen on her knees, facing the dusty fireplace, Craig at her side, doing the same. After several minutes of silence, she finally heard the men whispering to each other farther away, somewhere in the kitchen, but she couldn't make out what they were saying.

She felt Craig's fingers carefully reach for hers, working their way to interlock. A sign of camaraderie. He whispered almost inaudibly, "I'll get us out of this. They're wearing masks, which means they don't need to kill us."

She stayed silent, staring at the bricks along the fireplace. Finally, she heard the men approaching them, speaking in Spanish. Their words were too fast for her to mentally translate. She wondered if one of them was Hector.

"Please, you don't have to do this," Craig pleaded. The men were now right behind them. "I can get you the money. I swear. Please don't hurt my wife. She's innocent."

Craig, you're going to get us killed. Just shut up.

"Time's up, *ese*," the man replied. "We know you lost your job, and no longer have an income. Unless your old lady's got a secret stash of money laying around?" He pointed his gun at Blake as he addressed her. "Do you, bitch?"

Blake panicked. Her strategy had been to keep quiet, but now she was being forced to speak. "No," she finally whispered. "He stole it all."

The man erupted into laughter, clearly amused by this. "Damn, she's feisty!"

Craig searched her eyes, confused.

"I know everything," she said, meeting Craig's eyes with

rage and pain. "I know what you did to us."

He looked defeated, like he'd just lost the will to fight.

"Blake," he said, tears in his eyes. "I'm so sorry."

"Alright, that's enough talk," the man said. "Bag 'em."

Something dark was violently forced over her head and tied tight around her neck. Everything was black now. The material on her face was rough, like burlap. And while she felt like she was having a heart attack, she held still and stayed quiet.

"Please, I can fix this," Craig continued, his voice muffled now, like he had a bag over his head too. "Just don't—"

Fwepp. A quiet gunshot. The silencer.

Then silence.

Oh my god. Craig is dead. Her brain was burning and buzzing. *Craig is dead. This is how it ends. I let the bastard kill us.*

But then, after a moment, she heard Craig crying, sounds of excruciating pain.

Craig is alive. She silently cried, overwhelmed by this nightmare rollercoaster.

"Calm down, you pussy," one of the men said coldly. "It's just your leg. A warm-up shot."

They shot Craig in the leg.

"Now. You know why we're here," the man directly behind Blake said. "I need my money."

"I just...need a little...time." Craig was choking out his words, clearly in pain.

"You're out of time," the man replied.

"Where is Kendra?" Craig asked between whimpers. Blake was shocked to hear the name come out of his mouth in front of her. *He must really think this is the end.*

"Damn, homie, that's cold," one of the other men said.

"I thought you wanted to keep your little affair a secret," the man behind Blake said, laughing. "Isn't that why you traded that slut Kendra as collateral? So that your wife wouldn't find out what a piece of shit you are? What was the point if you were just gonna come clean right before you both die? If it were me, I'd have taken that shit to the grave."

Blake was no longer breathing. She was outside of her body, looking in, regretting so much of her life.

"Please don't kill my wife. Please just kill me." Craig's voice was softer now, like he was going into shock.

"*Ese*, you know it doesn't work that way," the man said coldly. "I told you I always collect my debts one way or another. Now. Ladies first."

Blake felt something hard press against the back of her head. *I'm not ready* was the only thought that passed through her brain.

"I changed my mind. Remove his hood," the man behind Blake said to his friends. "He should see this."

"PLEASE DON'T—DON'T DO THIS—PLEASE, PLEASE, PLEASE, GOD, NO, PLEASE." Craig was screaming, no longer muffled. She was surprised by her next thought in this moment: that she felt bad for Craig, that he had to see her with a bag over her head and a gun pointed at her skull. That he would have to watch her die. That he would watch her be murdered, knowing it was his fault.

She heard something click, and the gun was pushed harder into the back of her skull. She squeezed her eyes shut and braced herself, silently telling herself it would all be over soon, and that she wouldn't know the difference afterward. It would be nothingness. She would no longer feel. She would no longer be.

And then she heard a loud gunshot. A *pop.*

Dazed, she waited for the pain to come. Waited for darkness. *Am I dead?*

Then she heard another gunshot. Then another. *Pop. Pop. Pop.*

She felt the gun slip from the back of her head and heard a loud thud behind her.

The hood was pulled off her head, and she looked up to see Hayden smiling down at her.

"Hey, neighbor."

Chapter 17

Blake took in the scene around her. The room was still dark, but the sun was now rising outside, casting an early morning glow in the house. All three masked men lay lifeless on the living room floor, blood pooling out of them. Standing above them were Red, Dave, and Elvis. They looked harder than before. There was blood splattered on Red's usually adorably freckled face, and he had a dangerous look in his eye. Lying in a fetal position on the floor was Craig. His face was drained to a transparent white, and he was holding his wounded leg, unsuccessfully attempting to keep it sealed. Blood seeped out around his fingers as he rocked back and forth, clearly in shock.

An arm was suddenly around her waist, and she felt herself being lifted off the floor to her feet.

"You ok?" Hayden asked as he helped steady her. Once she was stable, he stuck his gun into the back of his jeans.

"I..." she started, unable to form words.

Hayden pulled her into his arms. "Dave, Elvis," he called. "Go get something to stop the bleeding." He gestured to Craig on the floor.

Dave and Elvis obeyed, quickly collecting towels and Blake's first aid kit to help Craig. Craig yelped in pain as Elvis poured hydrogen peroxide on his bloody knee.

"Oh, calm down," Elvis said. "You should feel grateful to be alive right now. There's an exit wound, so the bullet went straight through. That'll make this easier to patch up."

As the Army of Outlaws tended to Craig's wound, Blake felt all the sensations come back into her body, and she was finally able to find words.

"You killed them," Blake said to Hayden, looking up at him from under his arm.

"They were going to kill you," he said automatically.

"But how did you know?" she asked. "I thought you were off on a ride," and before she could stop herself, "and don't you hate me now?"

"The ride was to follow these assholes," he said, gently stroking her cheek. "And they led us straight to you. And as for the 'hating you' thing, if you think that's the first time Christina's gotten jealous and told me lies about another girl, then you've got a lot to learn, sweetheart." He tilted his head playfully at her as he took in her outfit. "Nice sushi pajamas, by the way."

In that moment, Blake was overcome with relief, gratitude, admiration. This was what a real man was, in her eyes. Someone who would do whatever it took to handle a situation. Without thinking, she leaned in and kissed Hayden hard on the lips. Though momentarily stunned, he kissed her back, pulling her body into his and running his fingers through her hair.

When they finally pulled away from each other, she opened her eyes and looked around at the scene again. Red was on his phone in the backyard. Dave was ripping up one of her bedsheets, presumably to create a bandage, and Elvis was running a flame from his lighter along the edge of one of her kitchen knives. Craig was staring straight at her, his face locked in utter confusion and terror. His eyes searched hers for answers, clearly overwhelmed by the trauma of the situation. She knew he was trying to make sense of what he'd just experienced: watching his wife make out with their outlaw next-door neighbor who'd just killed everyone in the house, everyone who'd been about to murder them. He opened his mouth to say something, but at that moment, Red re-entered the room.

"Squad is on the way to come handle cleanup," he said, walking toward Dave and Elvis.

"Good," Hayden said, walking over to the group and leaving Blake behind. "Alright, Red, you take that side. I'll take his legs."

"What the hell are you doing?" Craig screamed as the Army of Outlaws pinned him down.

"Hold still," Elvis ordered. Hayden, Red, and Dave used force to hold Craig steady. Without warning, Elvis took the searing hot blade that he'd been burning for the past few minutes and pressed it hard into Craig's bullet wound. Craig's scream rattled the entire house. And then Elvis did the same thing to the exit wound. More screams. Blake watched in silence as the men cauterized his wound.

"You're ok, man," Red said to Craig when it was over, while Dave was wrapping the makeshift bandage around his leg. "Now you don't need to go to the hospital."

"Who are you people?" Craig finally asked them, after his shock was apparently wearing off and he was more aware of where he was.

"We're the guys who just saved your wife's life," Hayden said to him. "Now, I'm sorry to do this while you're injured, but my friends are gonna have to take you with them."

Dave and Elvis launched the injured Craig to his feet, zip tying his hands behind his back and supporting his bound arms on either side to help him walk.

"What?" Craig looked afraid. "What are you doing?"

"Yeah, what?" Blake asked, confused.

But Hayden didn't make eye contact with Blake or acknowledge her question. Instead, he grabbed her hand and squeezed it, silently cautioning her, while his friends led Craig toward the back door. Craig was still confused, asking where they were taking him, but he seemed too weak to struggle. Hayden nodded as Red closed the back door behind his friends, who were supporting the limping Craig and escorting him away in zip ties. Now Blake and Hayden were alone with the three dead bodies, whose blood was now spreading and soaking through the hardwood floors.

"Are you gonna tell me what's going on?" Blake asked, still reeling. She couldn't stop staring at the bodies. "Where are you taking him?"

"Why are you so worried about it?" Hayden asked, suddenly cold. "You were almost just murdered in cold blood because of him."

"Yeah, but..." She felt too weak to struggle or argue.

"Listen," he said angrily, letting go of her hand. "You see this?" He pointed down at the dead bodies on her hardwood floor. "These are Desperados. *Were* Desperados."

"I picked up on that," she said solemnly.

"Do you understand what it means that three Desperados are now dead, murdered—by me—in your house?"

She was silent, waiting for him to continue.

"It means the Army of Outlaws just started a war with them. If they find out it was us who killed him, they will retaliate.

And Hector has the resources to really fuck us." He was angry. "We've had a truce for the past four years, and it's been shaky at best. This will end that truce."

"I'm sorry," Blake said, placing her hands on Hayden's chest. "I owe you my life. And I'm so sorry you had to break your truce to save it."

"You owe me nothing," he said, still cold. She removed her hands from his chest, alarmed, as he continued. "You did the club a favor when you locked Robert back into the shed. You helped us out, so we helped you out tonight. Now we're even."

"Oh," she said, feeling hurt. "Glad we're even then."

She heard motorcycles firing up and commotion happening outside next door. "Where are they taking Craig?"

"He has to stand trial."

"What?" She knew what that had meant for Robert, and what it could mean for Craig. "I thought you said we're even?"

"*You* and the club are even. Your husband is not. He's the one that started this mess. He's the reason we had to intervene and kill these Desperados." He gestured again to the dead bodies. "Now, we decide his fate."

"But can't you just let him go? He's...so sad. He won't hurt anyone." She hated Craig, but she didn't want him to die.

"I don't understand why you're defending him," Hayden shot back. "He cheated on you and would have gotten you killed if I didn't get here in time."

"And I'm so grateful to you, Hayden. Really. It's just...he's been my husband for years. I want him out of my life; I don't want him dead."

"Unfortunately, that's not how it works, sweetheart. A debt is a debt. It's gotta be paid."

You sound just like that Desperado, right before he was about to murder me.

"What am I supposed to do in the meantime?" She felt defeated, disillusioned, disappointed, tired. She just wanted to sleep. More motorcycles swarmed into the driveway next door, perforating her eardrum with their deafening engines.

"For starters, you can come with me," he ordered, looking out the window. "Go get dressed and pack a bag. We're going away for the night."

"But, what about them?" she asked, gesturing to the bodies on her living room floor. She felt her stomach turn as she noticed the bullet wound in the chest of the Desperado who'd held a gun to her head. She was grateful that they all still had their masks on, so she didn't have to see their dead faces.

"Give me a key to your house so my friends can clean this up."

The alarm. The thought pummeled her. *Did I not actually turn it on last night? Better make sure it's off before Hayden's friends come.*

She headed to her bedroom, where the traumatic night had commenced, to pack a bag as Hayden had instructed. She was afraid of him now. He'd been so cold, so pragmatic, so devoid of empathy. But the fate of Craig now laid in Hayden's hands, and she needed to tread carefully. Plus, it appeared her only other option was to stay there with three dead bodies, and she much preferred the alternative of riding off somewhere safe with Hayden while someone else came over to clean up the mess.

They rode in silence on Hayden's motorcycle for what seemed like half a day. It was probably only a couple of hours, but holding on for dear life on the back of a bike somehow made the time pass more slowly. Her bag was packed in the storage compartment, and she was dressed like she was in mourning: black faux-leather leggings, black boots, black tank top, black denim jacket. Her blonde hair was loose under the Bitch Helmet, whipping her in the face. The sting of the wind in her eyes was almost a welcome sensation, giving her something to focus on besides the previous night of horrors. When they finally exited the 101 freeway, they cruised into another beautiful beach town along the Central Coast. She saw a sign that said CAMBRIA and realized they were more than two hours north of Ventura. She'd researched Cambria when they'd first moved to Ventura, bookmarking it as a fun day trip for her and Craig, complete with numerous sea lions sunbathing on the beach and the famous Hearst Castle.

Hayden pulled into a quaint-looking motel off the main ocean-front road.

"Wait here," he instructed, dismounting the bike, and walking toward the on-site office.

She felt her phone vibrate in her denim jacket pocket and pulled it out to swipe open.

Detective Vasquez: Everything ok over there?

Her heart stopped.

"I got us a key, lady," Hayden called to her from across the courtyard. "Get your bag and come over here."

"Coming!" she shouted back. She looked down at her text from Vasquez.

Blake: All good here!

Once the text was sent, she quickly deleted the conversation.

Please don't text me again today.

Entering their room at the cabin-style motel along the coastal road, Blake inferred that the place was meant for couples. There was a cozy queen bed, a working fireplace, and an oversized jacuzzi tub in the bathroom. Under different circumstances, where she hadn't just nearly escaped death and her husband wasn't being held prisoner by the man she'd come here with, this place might feel like a romantic getaway.

"Let me show you the view," Hayden whispered into her ear as she set her overnight bag down on the plush, purple chair next to the bed. His whisper gave her chills. Even though a significant part of her was afraid of him and what he was capable of, she still found herself illogically infatuated. They walked down the little road from their room toward the bluffs. The clouds above cast a striking landscape of grey, moody skies colliding with the dark blue, murky ocean, which formed waves that crashed forcefully into the base of the cliffs. There was no beach down below, seemingly high tide. Something about this picturesque, dark scene made her feel uneasy. What was going to happen to Craig? What was going to happen with those dead Desperados? And what was going to happen to her?

"You cold?" Hayden asked after they'd stared at the ocean in silence for several minutes, snapping her out of her trance. She realized she was visibly shivering under her denim jacket.

"A little."

"Let's get you warmed up."

He was acting surprisingly warm toward her, a drastic shift from his emotionless, all-business demeanor that morning, when he'd told her that her husband would need to stand trial. She'd watched him stand over the bodies of men he'd murdered in cold blood (albeit to save her life), and she didn't see even the tiniest glimmer of remorse or distress. He seemed unaffected by it, like it was normal for him. *How many people has Hayden killed?* But she didn't have anyone else she could rely on. Craig had traded Kendra as collateral, whatever that meant. She wasn't sure she wanted to know. Was Kendra still alive? All she knew was that all the men surrounding her did bad things, and at this point she was focused on survival. Siding with the lesser of two evils.

And then there was Detective Vasquez. He seemed to be the only man in her life with good intentions, despite his odd and unprofessional behavior. He'd helped her through this dark time, tried to protect her. But now she'd have to cut him out too. She couldn't tell him the truth about what happened at her house. He was police. There was no way she could divulge the truth without implicating Hayden and his club. They'd never be able to prove it was self-defense. Hayden's friends cutting off identifiable features and torching the bodies would see to that. *I'll have to keep this to myself, at least until after they let Craig go and we figure out how to move forward from all of this.*

Blake felt the chill deepening in her body once they were back inside, the warmth of the room not helping to offset her shivering.

"Sit here. I'm going to draw you a bath," Hayden said, much to her surprise. She didn't argue. She was sleep deprived and traumatized, and felt the stress and fatigue in her bones. She nodded to him as he turned toward the bathroom. A few minutes later, he re-emerged with a bathrobe and towel in hand. Behind him, there was dim mood lighting and the comforting noise of hot water filling the gigantic tub.

"These are for you," he said, handing her the robe and towel. "I'm gonna run a quick errand. Be back in a few, ok?"

He was leaving her again. This time though, she didn't mind it. She felt the hot bath calling to her and was relieved to have a few minutes of privacy.

"Ok." She smiled weakly at him.

After he left, locking the door behind him, she ventured into the bathroom and saw, to her pleasant surprise, that there were bubbles in the bath. She smiled even though she knew she shouldn't. She should be angry and afraid. But all she felt was the bath calling to her. Eager to warm her body up, she ripped off all her clothes, kicking them into a pile on the cold, ceramic-tiled floor, and sunk her whole body into the tub. Instant calm. She closed her eyes and let the water soak into her tired skin. Just a few short minutes later, the door to the room opened.

That was quick. Then, instant fear. *Too quick.*

"Hayden?" She inched toward the edge of the tub to stabilize herself, frantically searching for a weapon, just in case. She stupidly grabbed a metal box of tissues, holding it protectively.

"I'm back," Hayden replied from the bedroom. *Oh, thank God.* She sank back into the tub, heart racing. *Maybe I am traumatized.*

"That was fast," she said, calming herself.

"It was a quick errand."

She heard glassware clinking, and then Hayden emerged, holding a bottle of wine and two glasses. He set the glasses down on the bathroom counter, pulling a corkscrew out of his jeans pocket to open the bottle. She stared up at him silently as he performed this unexpected romantic act: drawing her a bath and feeding her wine in the tub. She didn't know how to feel. She lusted after him in a way that she'd never felt before. But he was also a real-life murderer and gang member who was keeping her husband as his prisoner.

Hayden poured her a glass and handed it to her in the tub. He lingered above her, looking down into the water, beyond the bubbles. His lips curled into a mischievous smile.

"What?" she asked, blushing.

"You look pretty when you're vulnerable."

She smiled at this. She couldn't hold back anymore. He'd found a way to knock down her protective walls. "So, are you just gonna stare at me all night, or are you gonna join me in here?"

"I thought you'd never ask," he said, setting his wine glass down on the counter. Shaking out of his cut, he laid it gently on a dry part of the counter, before aggressively pulling his t-shirt off and unbuckling his belt. She watched hungrily from the bathtub, hiding behind the bubbles and wine. As he slid effortlessly into the bathtub with her, she felt safe again. *Maybe if we just stay here, in this cozy little cottage, things will be ok. Let's just shut out the world.*

Hayden grabbed her legs under the water's surface and pulled her across the tub into his lap. She could feel how hard he was, pressed into her lower back. But he didn't make a move right away. Instead, he grabbed a washcloth and gently washed her. Occasionally, he'd kiss her ear or neck, but he primarily focused on bathing her. It was the most intimate moment they'd shared in the weeks they'd known each other. It was raw and vulnerable. All cards on the table, all truths out, all clothes off. Naked physically and emotionally. Nothing to hide behind.

Hayden must have sensed she'd reached her peak of antici-pation and unsatisfied desire, because he finally gave in. He let go of the washcloth, moving to massage her shoulders with his fingertips. Slowly, he glided his fingers down her arms, down the tops of her thighs, and then inward. She exhaled deeply as he kissed her neck and touched her intimately. How could this gangster be so gentle with her? How could these conflicting worlds slide so easily in and out of one another, between violence and love making, between murder and sex? She let herself go completely, under Hayden's spell, forgetting about the fatal holes he'd shot into the men in her house, and about how he'd taken her husband prisoner, and about how he'd choked her and shown her a violent side of himself, and about how his friend Rocco had tried to rape her. There was only the present, the right now, the *moment.* When Hayden pulled her out of the tub to fuck her on the bed in front of the now kindled fire, she was completely and irrevocably his. His to love. His to use.

Hayden held her in his arms for a long time afterward, and she felt her anxiety and fears slowly creep back in as the physical high from Hayden wore off.

"What's going to happen to Craig?" she asked quietly. She couldn't get the thought of him badly injured, traumatized, and now locked up somewhere out of her mind.

"Depends."

"On?"

"What the council decides."

"Aren't you part of the council?"

"Yes."

"So, you have a vote, right?"

"Yes."

"Can you..." She was frustrated that he was making her work so hard. "Can you maybe advocate for showing him mercy?"

"And why would I do that?"

"Because I'm asking you to?"

"And what makes you think I'd do something just because

you asked?"

"Because..." She trailed off. "You care about me."

"That's true. I do care about you," he agreed. "But the club is my world, my law. It's everything. My loyalty is to my brothers. If eliminating your worthless, piece-of-shit husband is the right thing for the club, then I will back that decision. If showing him mercy is the right thing to do, then I'll get behind that."

I wonder if he'd still feel loyal if he knew his buddy Rocco tried to rape me. She contemplated telling him, but something deep inside her told her she wouldn't like the response, or the potential fallout. She couldn't trust Hayden. She knew that now. Hayden wasn't *good*. Unconsciously, she hardened in his arms, and could tell he sensed it.

"Don't worry, sweetheart," he said, returning to his usual arrogant and flirty self. "Right now, I'm feeling merciful. Maybe it has something to do with this banging body pressed up against me."

He kissed the top of her head, and they continued to lie there in silence. She was terrified of what he'd just said to her, fearing the worst-case scenario: becoming a widow at the hand of her lover. She prayed Hayden cared for her enough that he wouldn't do something that wicked to her. She had to hold onto hope that this would all work out. Eventually, she felt herself giving into her exhaustion and drifting off into a dreamworld, anchored to reality by Hayden's arms wrapped around her.

When she awoke, it took her a moment to remember where she was. Slowly opening her eyes, she absorbed the scene around her: a few embers still burning in the fireplace, clothes scattered all over the bathroom floor, a warm arm draped over her hip. She gently rolled over to face the man holding her.

Hayden was still asleep. He was so beautiful, like he'd been carved out of marble. His strong jawline and full lips made him look like a movie star, but his shadowy start of a beard and shaggy, long hair that always seemed to be a little dirty gave him that rougher, outlaw appearance.

Gingerly, like she was playing the board game Operation, she untangled her body from his, separating herself to sneak out of the bed without waking him. She quietly grabbed her overnight bag and tiptoed into the bathroom, pressing the door closed behind her. After she finished brushing her teeth and washing her face, she shut off the water, and in the new silence heard Hayden talking quietly in the bedroom. She pressed her ear up against the door to listen.

"No, man. This is a delicate situation. And there's no reason we need to execute him as long as the Desperados can't tie us to their dead amigos."

He was quiet for a moment, listening to whoever was on the other end of his phone call.

"I don't care about the fucking cops in the neighborhood. Our orders are to keep him in the backyard."

The backyard. Did he mean...the shed? Did they lock Craig up in that place? She was overcome with anxiety, thinking about a new Man in the Shed. Her husband. But she latched onto a newfound sense of hope from hearing Hayden say there was no need to kill Craig if no one found out the Army of Outlaws was responsible for the murders of their three club members.

"Later, bro."

She waited a moment before re-entering the bedroom, pretending not to have overheard his phone conversation.

"Hey," she said.

"Hey, gorgeous." He smiled at her. He was still under the

covers, and she longed to climb back in with him. But as she silently debated whether that was a good idea, he shot out of bed and walked to the bathroom in all his naked glory, shutting the door behind him.

She took this opportunity to pull fresh clothes out of her bag and get dressed. But as she stepped into a pair of jeans, she heard her phone vibrate. Her breath caught in her throat when she read a new text from Vasquez.

> *Detective Vasquez: Are you still ok? I heard three Desperados went missing. Just worried about you.*

> *Blake: Still ok. Thank you for checking on me. {smiling emoji}*

Hayden returned to the bedroom, fully dressed, as she slid her phone back into her purse.

"You ready to head out?" he asked, gathering his belongings.

"Yeah," she said, shoving her previous day's clothes into the bag and zipping it shut. "Have you heard anything about Craig?"

Hayden didn't respond but picked up her bag and slung it over his shoulder.

"What about my house?" She tried a hopefully less controversial question.

"Your house is clean. You're good to go home now."

"Thanks," she said, still unsatisfied. "Can you just tell me something—anything—about what happens next?"

"You hungry?" he asked energetically. "I'm starving. Let's get breakfast burritos." With that, they left the motel and saddled up on his motorcycle for the long ride home.

Chapter 18

Blake paced back and forth in her living room, her eyes locking in on the three spots on the floor where only 24 hours prior, there had been dead bodies. She inspected the room and didn't find so much as a drop of blood or stray hair. The house was clean. Hayden hadn't come inside with her when they'd returned home, clearly confident in his friends' work and not feeling the need to check it. She didn't want to admit it to him, but she was afraid of being home alone in this house. She'd never believed in ghosts, but she'd also never lived in a house where people had been murdered. It was unsettling. And the fact that she'd just survived a home invasion there didn't help.

She also found herself obsessing over whether Craig was now locked up in the shed next door. She hated this purgatory of not knowing. She no longer felt safe anywhere or with anyone. Not wanting to be alone with her thoughts and the ghosts of gangsters, she dialed Jasmine's number.

"Blake!" Jasmine screamed through the phone at her. "Where have you been?"

"I know, I'm so sorry I've been MIA," Blake apologized. "There's been a lot going on."

"Is everything ok?"

"Not really," Blake replied honestly. "I'm in trouble. Craig is...missing."

She took a deep breath and filled her friend in, leaving out the parts where she'd aided the Army of Outlaws and where the Desperados had been murdered in her home. She didn't want to risk dragging Jasmine into the fold of gang violence, and figured the less Jasmine knew about the situation, the safer she would be. She did, however, explain that Craig had been gambling, that this wasn't the first time he'd been gambling, and that he'd gotten mixed up with a gang to whom he owed money and now was missing. She twisted the truth a bit to protect Hayden and ultimately to protect Jasmine. But she did allow herself to unload the dark secret that had been weighing on her and finally say the words out loud: she and Craig were both having affairs.

"What about the police?" Jasmine asked, almost breathless.

Fuck. Vasquez knows the Desperados are missing. I wonder what else he knows. I wonder if the other Desperados know what happened to their friends.

Before she could respond, she heard motorcycles firing up next door. She peeked out the window and saw Hayden and gang getting ready to leave the house.

"Hellooooo? You there?" Jasmine's voice called through the phone.

"Yeah, sorry about that," Blake replied, now distracted. "Hey, can I call you back in a little bit?"

"Famous last words."

"I know, I know. I promise this time!"

After they hung up, Blake impulsively grabbed her purse and snuck out front, hiding behind the border of bushes that separated their properties.

"Dave, you're riding with the detainee," Hayden ordered.

"Where's Red?"

"Haven't seen him since this morning," Dave replied.

"Alright, Elvis, you go with him."

Dave and Elvis climbed into the same black car she'd seen the day they'd kidnapped Robert and imprisoned him in the shed. *Is Craig in that car?* Hayden and two other men hopped on their motorcycles and drove away down the street. Once they were out of sight, Blake sprinted to her car and turned on the engine, preparing to follow the Army of Outlaws.

She tailed them for 20 minutes, leaving enough space to prevent any suspicion, but staying close enough to successfully keep them in view. Finally, the pack of motorcycles and cars turned down an unmarked road into the woods, and she followed them into a rural oasis, surrounded by almost 360 degrees of sky-high mountains. They'd ventured so far into the wilderness that she could no longer see any signs of civilization around them. They were off the grid. She slowed her car to a stop when she saw them park and shut off their engines in a clearing that bordered a cluster of crowded trees. There was at least a dozen more motorcycles and Outlaws already there, waiting for Hayden's group. Carefully, she put her car in reverse, pulling it backward around a corner to hide it behind a tall hill, and then parked and crept toward the group on foot.

Once she reached a cluster of trees near the gathering, she hid behind a particularly girthy oak tree. She was in ear and eye shot but prayed there was enough distance to keep herself hidden.

"Hayden, how are the amigos?" a tall, scary, older man said. He had a short buzz cut and a long, silver beard and was wearing his cut over a tank top so that his substantial biceps were on full display. The group of 20 or so men were slowly but surely forming a large semicircle around where Hayden stood next to the black car.

"Amigos are taken care of. Red, Jesse, and Big Dog took point on garbage disposal duty," Hayden said.

"They better do it right this time. We can't have fucking bodies washing up again."

"Don't worry. These bodies will never be discovered."

"Good," the scary man said. Blake wondered if this was the president. He spoke to Hayden with a sense of authority that she hadn't seen the other guys use. "Now where is this sonofabitch who's the reason we're gathered here today?"

Hayden tapped the window of the black car, and the doors flew open. Dave and Elvis emerged, pulling Craig out of the car.

Craig. You poor idiot. I'll get you out of this. And then I'll divorce your ass.

Craig had bruises on his face, like he'd been punched repeatedly, and his hands were still bound behind his back. He was also still in his pajamas from the night of the break in, and he looked unwashed and frazzled.

"There he is!" the scary man with the buzz cut said. "The man of the hour."

Dave shoved Craig forward, an order to move closer to the man addressing him. Craig slowly walked forward toward the middle of the semicircle of Outlaws. All eyes were on him.

"So, you're the guy who's causing our club all this drama," he said to Craig. "I really don't like drama."

Craig stood there silently, his face locked in fear.

"He's a piece of shit, yes," Hayden chimed in. "But no one besides us knows what happened to those Desperados. He's not going to be a liability anymore."

"How can you guarantee that? Just because you killed the

men he owed doesn't make the debt go away. They'll just send other amigos to collect."

"So why don't we exile him? Make him go back to Arizona where he came from, so he's someone else's problem."

Hayden is trying to save Craig's life.

"That's very noble of you, Hayden. But we're all aware of your relationship to his family. We can't just change our rules because you're fucking his wife."

Craig recoiled at this statement, clearly upset.

"I'm just trying to keep our body count low this year, *Frank*," Hayden challenged. "We've already been drawing too much attention to the club."

A motorcycle zoomed past her and pulled up to the group. The rider took off his helmet. It was Red, covered from head to toe in red blood.

Hayden, Dave, and Elvis immediately ran over to their friend.

"Red, are you ok?" Hayden asked frantically, helping him off his bike to stand. "What happened?"

"Desperados," Red shouted in between struggled short breaths, blood spewing from his mouth. "They know."

"What?" Hayden looked terrified. "How?"

"I don't know," Red replied, blood dripping from his injured face. "But somehow they know it was us. They only let me live so that I could relay the message to you all. They're declaring war on the Outlaws. They're coming for us."

Blake felt her heart stop and all the blood rush out of her core.

"Well, now we have our answer!" Frank declared, his eyes wild. "Looks like this motherfucker *is* a liability."

Hayden was silent, holding his forehead between his middle finger and thumb in deep thought.

"Better to be safe than sorry," Frank continued.

"I'll do it." Rocco stepped into the circle and pulled his gun out of the back of his pants, clicking off the safety.

"No," Frank said. "As much as I admire your love of murdering people, it needs to be Hayden."

Rocco reluctantly put his gun back into his pants and walked back toward the outer group.

"Why does it have to be me?" Hayden was incredulous.

"Because you're going to be president someday, and you need to learn discipline," Frank replied. *So, Hayden is being groomed.* "You don't get to *not* shoot someone who needs to be shot just because you like the way his wife sucks your dick, and because you feel bad for the guy."

"That's not what this is about," Hayden said. "We are supposed to hold a fair trial before we decide someone's fate. That's part of our manifesto."

"Tell me something," Frank replied. "How could the Desperados possibly know it was us that hit their amigos? Hmm? The only witnesses were club members, that girl you're fucking, and her husband. Someone ratted us out. Who was it?"

"I don't know," Hayden said, sounding less defensive and more defeated now.

"Honestly, I'd rather kill both of them and just be done with it. But I'm sparing the girl because of what she did for the club, locking that cocksucker Robert back up when he tried to escape. For that, she gets to keep her life. For now. But this guy? His time is up."

Please do something, Hayden. Please just let Craig go.

A hand landed hard on her shoulder and she screamed. All biker eyes looked up from the trial and stared directly at her. She turned around to see Rocco facing her.

"Look what I found!" he shouted through her to his friends

in the clearing. "Looks like this curious little cat wanted to witness her husband's execution. Come on, woman."

Rocco pushed her hard, sending her into a run to stop herself from falling forward. She looked up and met Hayden's eyes. He looked utterly disappointed.

"Did this bitch follow you here?" Frank asked Hayden, as Rocco nudged Blake into their circle.

"Apparently," Hayden said.

"You're off your game," Frank scolded. "How could you not notice a dumb blonde on your tail?"

Hayden was silent.

"Alright, I'm getting bored," Frank declared. "Time to end this."

"Oh my god," Craig muttered, starting to cry.

"Wait!" Blake screamed. "You don't have to do this."

"Shut that bitch up," Frank said. Dave and Rocco swooped in and held her by the arms. Hayden shook his head sadly at her as he pulled his gun out of his pants.

"Hayden, don't!" she yelled.

Rocco slapped her across the face. "The president just said to shut the fuck up, bitch."

Craig turned to Blake, stoic now. "It's ok, Blake. I deserve this. This is the way it has to be. You'll be ok. I promise."

Hayden stepped forward, gun in hand.

"Get down on your knees," he instructed Craig. Craig did as Hayden told him. "Face the other way." Craig looked up at him, eyes wide. "Don't worry, man. I'll make it quick. I promise."

"You don't have to do this!" Blake screamed, unable to restrain herself.

Rocco slammed his elbow into her face, and her vision went black for a moment. And as it returned and the scene in front

216

of her came into focus, she watched Hayden point his gun at the back of Craig's head as Craig faced away from them. And then he pulled the trigger.

Chapter 19

Blake opened her eyes to a blurry scene, trying to make sense of her surroundings. After blinking a few times, she realized she was staring at her bedroom ceiling. *How did I get here?*

"Hey, sweetheart," Hayden said as he entered the room, carrying a glass of water. He set it down on the bedside table next to her.

"What happened?" she asked, confused.

"You fainted...er passed out...back in the woods. I carried you and drove you home. You slept the entire night."

It all came crashing back. Craig. The execution.

"Is Craig...dead?"

"Yes."

"Oh god," she said, her stomach turning. She launched herself out of bed and ran to the bathroom, vomiting into the toilet.

"I'm so sorry, Blake," Hayden said genuinely as he followed her to bathroom. "I know you can't forgive me right now, but I hope you can at least understand it."

Blake looked up from her kneeling position at the toilet and met Hayden's blue eyes. Seeing his face triggered the memory of him pulling the trigger at the back of Craig's head, murdering him in front of her. She gagged and vomited more. When she was finally done, Hayden moved in and lifted her from the floor, helping her to her feet. She could no longer look him in the eyes. Doing so caused a visceral, painful response.

"Are you ok?" he asked as he helped her back into her bed. "Rocco hit you pretty hard."

"What do you think?" she asked angrily.

"Listen," he said, sitting next to her on the bed. "You may not want to hear this, but you need to. We're gonna pin Craig's death on the Desperados. We have enough evidence to point the police in that direction, which means they shouldn't come after you or question you. But you need to listen carefully to these details so that your story is consistent with what happened to him."

She didn't respond, but nodded her head, ready to listen. Hayden told her the story of how Craig died at the hands of the Desperados, to whom he owed money, and how they finally came to collect their debt. His body would be found soon in a back alley near the casino. The crime scene would be consistent with a Desperados-style execution, and the police would have the evidence they needed to pin the Mexican motorcycle club. Hayden hoped that this would also mislead the surviving Desperados to think that their missing club members were somehow tied to Craig's murder, throwing them off the scent and obfuscating the truth.

"Ok," she finally said, after Hayden finished his long speech.

"Ok," he echoed. "There's one other thing. Another big thing. I think you should leave town."

"What?" She was surprised by this. *Hayden wants to get rid of me.* Though she could no longer look into his eyes without wanting to puke, the rejection still stung.

"It's not safe for you here," he said gently. "If you stay here,

I can't guarantee I can protect you. Your best chance is going back to Phoenix."

"Well, I guess I don't really have a reason to stay here now anyway," she said coldly.

"Do you have someone you can go stay with?"

"Yep." Colder.

"Ok, well I'm gonna let you rest, sweetheart. I'll be next door if you need anything."

She nodded but didn't say anything more. And then he left. She was all alone in the murder house. She was all alone in the world. And then her phone buzzed.

Vasquez was calling her.

"Hello?"

"Blake," Vasquez said seriously. "We need you to come down to the station. Something...bad has happened. Can you come right away?"

That was fast.

She saw her car keys on the kitchen counter and parked car in the driveway. Hayden must have driven her home in her own car. She grabbed the keys and her purse and headed to the police station.

When she entered the Ventura police headquarters, she immediately spotted Vasquez, wearing a fitted black suit, surrounded by police officers in uniform. She'd forgotten how intimidating he looked when he was dressed up. Intimidating but handsome. He watched her enter and gestured with his hand for her to approach him.

"Mrs. Davis," he greeted her formally. "Please follow us in here."

She was ushered into a private room with a conference table and chairs. Vasquez and his squad followed her into the room.

"Please have a seat," he said. He sat down across from her, while the other officers remained standing along the back wall.

"Mrs. Davis," he said solemnly. "I'm afraid we have some terrible news."

She sat there silently, waiting for the news she already knew.

"I'm afraid...your husband has been killed."

She let the emotions that had been building inside of her all afternoon surface in this moment, allowing herself to react appropriately to the news that her husband had been murdered. She covered her mouth with her hand as tears spilled from her eyes.

"No," she muttered, feigning shock.

"I know this must be devastating to hear," he said, reaching his hand across the table to gently place it on hers. The intimacy startled her, and she recoiled her hand, placing it in her lap.

"What happened?" she choked out, tapping into her real emotions to continue the façade of surprise.

"It appears he was mixed up with a gang in town and owed them money. When he couldn't pay...they took action. I'm so, so sorry."

"Can I see him?" she asked.

"Not right now, unfortunately," he said. "He's with Homicide, so we can't let you see him until they finish their report for the investigation.

Homicide. It was surreal hearing that word come from a detective's mouth to describe what happened to her husband. Even though she'd witnessed his murder, it just sounded so cold, so clinical, so removed.

Vasquez and the other police talked more as they instructed her to sign some forms, but her brain blocked most of it out. She just wanted to be out of that room and out of the station.

Finally, after what seemed like hours, they let her go home.

Once inside her house, she closed all the curtains on her windows, locked every lock, turned on the alarm, and pounded an entire bottle of wine until she got sleepy enough to pass out. In the morning, she was relieved to see she'd made it through the night. Bracing herself, she reached for her phone and dialed Jasmine's number.

After a two-hour phone call discussing the bleak news of Craig's death, Jasmine helped Blake make plans to move back to Phoenix. The plan was for Blake to crash with Jasmine for a little while until she got back on her feet, and then find herself a place in town. During this time, Jasmine was going to reach out to her real estate friend to help Blake sell her house in Ventura. Jasmine had also arranged for movers to come help pack up and move Blake's things. She'd always been good at organization and taking charge in stressful situations, and Blake was relieved to let her take over project management.

Soon after her call with Jasmine, Blake's phone blew up with calls and texts. Jasmine had commenced the phone tree so that Blake wouldn't have to. First Mom and Dad, then Craig's stepmom and dad, then Craig's sister in Dallas. She wasn't ready to talk to anyone yet, but she knew she'd have to face them sooner or later.

But while she was blatantly ignoring a new surge of incoming texts from family and friends, Vasquez suddenly called her.

"Hi," she breathed into the phone.

"Hi, Blake. How are you holding up?" he asked. "Actually, that's a stupid question. Don't answer that. Anyway, I don't mean to interrupt your grieving but...I just got word from my team, and if you want to go see him and say goodbye now, you can. He's at the Ventura County Medical Examiner's Office."

Her stomach flipped. *Oh god. Craig's body.* "Ok."

"I'll text you the information," he said gently. "Do you have someone who can go with you?"

"I'll be ok," she said quietly.

"It's good to lean on loved ones during a time like this," he lectured.

"I'll be ok," she repeated.

"Ok. There's one other thing. Can you stop by at 1 p.m. today?"

"For what?"

"Just some paperwork. We just have a few more questions, and there's a lawyer who wants to meet with you."

"A lawyer?" *Do they think I need a lawyer? Does that mean I'm a suspect?* She could barely breathe.

"It's nothing to worry about—just protocol, standard stuff."

"Ok," she said, trying to sound calm. "I'll be there."

At 1 p.m., she re-entered the police station in a hoodie pulled over her head and oversized sunglasses covering her face. Vasquez greeted her formally in a fresh, gray suit and led her to another similar room with a table and chairs.

"I wish I could hug you," he whispered to her as he shook her hand politely. "But with all these cops around it would be inappropriate."

She shrugged her shoulders, listless.

"Have a seat and help yourself to the water over there," he said, motioning to the cooler in the corner. "He'll be with you in just a moment."

"Ok," she said.

He nodded sympathetically and left the room.

After a few minutes, a short, pudgy man in a too-tight brown suit entered.

"Hello, Mrs. Davis," he said, plopping down in a chair opposite her and placing his briefcase on the table. "Hal Scherl." He stuck his hand out for her to shake. She took his hand and shook politely.

"My deepest condolences for your loss," he said sympathetically. "I know this is terrible timing and that you are processing this devastating news, but I'm here to discuss an urgent matter with you."

"You're a lawyer?" she asked.

"Yes, a life insurance policy claims attorney to be exact."

"I'm confused."

"Your husband—your *late* husband—took out a rather large life insurance policy about a month ago. And since he passed away within the agreed upon term for the policy, the benefits are set to be granted."

"I don't understand. Craig had a life insurance policy?"

"Yes, and you're the beneficiary. It's quite a big sum—just under a quarter of a million."

Her heart skipped a beat. *Craig knew his death was coming. He knew he'd fucked up, and that the only way he could make things right was by leaving me with financial security.* Her brain flashed the image of Craig with a gun to his head telling her it was ok and that it had to be this way, and she realized he really was ok with dying. He knew it was inevitable. He'd possibly even hoped to die because it was the only way to right his wrongs.

She started to cry. Violently.

Hal Scherl opened his briefcase and pulled out a travel pack of tissues, handing them to her. "In my line of work, you have to come prepared."

She accepted the tissues and dabbed at her eyes, her diaphragm convulsing from tears.

"I'll respectfully leave you to grieve in just a moment. But if I could just get your signature on a few of these forms, we can process the paperwork to release your cash."

She signed the forms, and he thanked her for her time, exiting the room as gracefully as he could, apologizing profusely for bombarding her during this difficult time.

Before the door could close behind Hal Scherl, Vasquez re-entered the room, this time shutting the door behind him.

"Blake," he said. "How can I help you? Can I get you anything? Coffee? Tea?"

"No," she said. "No, thank you. I don't know what I need right now. I feel numb."

"That's understandable," he said, sitting down at the table again. "Well, at least there's a silver lining, right?"

"What's that?"

"He didn't leave you in financial ruin."

"Oh," she said, surprised at the lack of attorney-client privilege. "I guess that lawyer told you about the life insurance?"

"I'm a cop." He smiled. "I'm good at getting things out of people."

"Yeah, I guess it's a silver lining. I'd prefer my husband to still be alive though."

"Of course. I'm so sorry. I didn't mean to be insensitive."

"It's ok," she said.

"Listen," he said, leaning inward. "It doesn't look great that your husband just took out that policy and then coincidentally died so soon after. There's a possibility you'll be under investigation."

"But I didn't even know about the policy until right now!"

"I know that, but the insurance company may not know that. This type of insurance fraud is very common, unfortunately.

225

But I'm filing a follow-up report for Craig's death this evening, and am going to put in writing that you've been cleared of any involvement or knowledge, ok?"

"Ok. Thanks. Can I go now?"

"Of course," he said, standing up from the table. "You should go home and rest. I'll walk you out."

The next morning, she lamented over whether to go see Craig's body. Part of her felt that was the right thing to do as his wife, but she was so overcome with guilt and shame that she didn't think she could bear it. Maybe a better sense of closure would come from leaving town immediately and retreating to the safety and comfort of her best friend. Her internal conflict was interrupted by her phone buzzing.

> *Detective Vasquez: Just checking on you. Are you taking care of yourself? Are you ok?*

> *Blake: I don't really know how I am. But I decided to move back to AZ for a bit until I figure out my next move.*

She waited for a minute, but he didn't respond, so she set her phone down. To distract herself from her anxiety and grief, she decided to begin packing. She blasted Radiohead through her speaker to drown out the world, and to drown out the motorcycles she heard next door. *I refuse to look.*

Chapter 20

The next morning, Blake awoke to her new reality, which was becoming more real with each day that passed. While she forced herself to resume packing up more of the house, Jasmine called her phone.

"Just checking on you, babe."

"I'm ok, actually. Making good progress on packing. I'm starting to feel a little more hopeful. I just want to be sitting on your couch drinking wine with you already."

"I stocked my house for you, so I'm ready to take care of you! The guest room is all set up, I have every kind of booze you could ever imagine, and tons of junk food for us to binge. We can be healthy bitches again soon, but I think comfort food is in order."

"Thank you," Blake said, tearing up. "I need a hug."

"I'll give you all the hugs!"

After a moment of silence, Jasmine followed up. "So...have they found out any more information yet? Are they going to arrest anybody?"

"I don't know," she said, walking to the garage to grab another box to pack. "All I know is they think it's this local gang, but I don't know if they're charging anyone yet."

"Have the police been looking after you? I'm worried for

your safety."

"Well, there's this detective who's been checking on me. He actually has been incredibly helpful. He came over last week and set up this whole security system for me."

Not that it mattered. The Desperados broke in anyway. She felt a strange sensation in her gut as she thought about this. *Did I really not turn the alarm on that night?*

"Wow, talk about full service," Jasmine said.

"Yeah. Hey, listen, I'm gonna go back to packing, but I'll call you tonight, ok?"

"Of course! I'm glad you're getting so much done. Remember, the movers will be there in two days!"

"I know. Can't wait. Love you."

"Love you too."

She set the phone down on a stack of storage bins as she reached to the top of a built-in shelving unit where the extra moving boxes were. But as she stood on her toes to knock the boxes down, she saw something that sent her flying backward in fear.

Wedged in between two storage bins near the ceiling was a tiny camera pointing right at her.

"What the fuck?" she asked out loud.

She grabbed a ladder from the other garage wall and set it up in front of the shelving unit. Climbing to the top, she reached out and grabbed the camera, snapping it from its affixed position, and climbing back down the ladder. She inspected it. There was no light on it, but she suspected it was on. *Like a nanny cam. Where did this come from?*

Panicked, she ran inside and scaled the interior of her house, searching for more cameras. Sure enough, when she reached the front entryway, she spotted another tiny camera nestled into her Ficus plant near the front door. *Ohmygod. Someone planted cameras in my fucking house.*

A terrifying question flew into her mind: How did the Desperados know that the Army of Outlaws were responsible for the murders of their three club members that happened in this house? The only people present were the Army of Outlaws, her, and Craig. Did someone *see* the murders through these cameras?

Then it hit her. *I know I turned that alarm on before bed the night the Desperados broke in.They must have had a code. Did... Vasquez...give them the code?*

He was the only other person who knew it, and he was the only person who'd been in her house before the night of the murders. She was panicking, her throat feeling like it was closing. It was Detective Vasquez all along. He was working with the Desperados.

And then she heard something clink in her kitchen. She grabbed a stray golf club from a pile of junk and slowly tiptoed toward the door to the kitchen. Once she passed the threshold, she scanned the room for intruders. Walking slowly with the club raised defensively, she peered around the corner.

"Is someone there?"

Something hard slammed into the back of her head, and her vision went black. The only sound she could hear was her own heart beating. And then, as her vision came back, a bag was violently shoved over her head, and someone kicked her in the back, sending her to her knees. She felt the burlap material being tightened and fastened at the neck. Then handcuffs slammed onto her wrists as her hands were forced behind her back.

"Hello, Blake," a man's voice said behind her. Vasquez.

"Sorry for hitting you. I really don't want to hurt you. But we can't have you leaving the state. Not when you're coming into all that money."

"It was you all along," Blake said quietly. "You're a Desperado."

"Eh, I'd say I'm more of a *friend of the club.*" Then he added, "But those guys your boyfriend murdered? Those were my cousins."

"But what about Sarah?" she asked desperately. "The Desperados murdered your girlfriend."

"You were being a suspicious bitch. I had to calm your ass down with something to make you trust me."

It was all a lie. She felt defeated. "What happens now?"

"Well, I'm going to help you pay off your debt," he said, helping her to her feet. "I think Kendra's getting pretty lonely. I'm sure she'll be thrilled to have a friend joining her."

Hayden, please be watching the house. Please see this.

"I'm gonna pull my car into your garage, so we can make this getaway real discreet. Don't you go anywhere while I'm gone."

She heard him go out the front door. As she stood there with a bag on her head and wrists handcuffed behind her back, she thought frantically about what she could possibly do in the limited time she had left. Quickly, with all the adrenaline and energy she had left inside of her, she walked, toes first to guide the way, toward where she'd left her phone. Finally, she felt the edge of the box where she'd set it down.

"Hey, Siri!"

Her iPhone dinged in response.

"Call H Money."

Siri faithfully replied, "Calling H Money."

The phone rang. And rang. And rang.

Come on, pick up. Pick up pick up pick up.

She heard the garage door opening.

Oh god, please pick up.

Hayden's voicemail.

A car was pulling into the garage.

Beep.

"Hayden, I'm being kidnapped. It's Detective Vasquez. He's a dirty cop. He's working with the Desperados. That's how they knew it was you who killed their friends. Please help m—"

Something hit her on the back of the head again, and she lost her balance, falling onto the floor.

"What did I just say about not going anywhere?" Vasquez said from somewhere above her. He lifted her off the ground and fireman-carried her through the garage, shoving her into the backseat of his car.

"Now, be a good girl and stay still. I told you, I don't want to hurt you."

She prayed that Hayden would get that voicemail, and that he cared enough to come save her. After everything, she hoped that maybe she could trust him. He was her only hope for survival.

About the Author

Amy Oppenheim is a marketing professional by day and writer by night. Her style is a culmination of an obsession with true crime and a love of all the charm the California Central Coast has to offer. A native Southern Californian, she has lived in Santa Barbara for over a decade and holds a B.A. in English Literature from the University of California, Santa Barbara.

You can connect with me on:
- https://www.amyjoppenheim.com
- https://twitter.com/AmyJeanneOpp

Made in the USA
Las Vegas, NV
01 October 2021

31501623R00142